P9-DEB-472

Chances Are

NO

A novel by Matthew Schofield

Dedicated to Cedric, Sophia, Genevieve and Brody, thanks for the inspiration. Dedicated to Claudia, thanks for the edit and encouragement.

Copyright © 2019 Matt Schofield

ISBN: 9781795107143

Independently published

Foreward

This piece of fiction is inspired by a news story I reported on in the mid-1990s while working for The Kansas City Star. It is, however, purely fictional in terms of events, names, the motivations of the killers and, well, everything except for inspiration. I realize in a Hollywood sense, this is a true "ripped from the headlines" sort of deal. It isn't in any real sense.

The real story involved two sets of spree killers, three in one group, two in the other, arriving within a few days of each other in a quiet small Missouri town. The first group kidnapped a man who had stopped to help them with their broken-down car while he was passing through town. They killed him a short time later, though a bit west across Missouri. The second group knocked on the door of longtime residents to ask for help. In total three people were murdered. The FBI classified it as "a bizarre coincidence."

The real story is horrifying, in the sense that real life murder is always horrifying. It's brutal and heartless and senseless. In the real story, the killers were simply killers.

This story tries to be horrifying in a way that horror stories are horrifying. The villains in this story are the result of my imagination. God help us if they aren't.

I did draw on my decades of writing about the human condition for this, however. I spent 35 years as a journalist. I was on the ground covering war in Iraq and Israel and Turkey and Ukraine. I spent the better part of a decade writing about terrorism, in France and Germany and England and Spain. I set foot in some 60 countries chasing after stories. I wrote for newspapers, and then newspaper websites. I wrote some long, multi-day pieces about crime, another about love, another about honor. I even spent a bit of time in Chernobyl writing about trying to make a life after a nuclear disaster.

Those were real life stories, true stories. This is a work of fiction. I made it up. I hope you like it.

Chapter 1

April 27 6:54 p.m.

Coach Karl Odin was lost in the developing artwork in front of him. Little streams of red curling through the black stubble on the back of Craig Johnson's young head. It was beautiful. Block out the rest of the world, block out the sounds of the traffic just down the ridge below him. Block out the howls of the coyotes, coyotes who would be quite useful in a few minutes. Block out the accelerated beating of his own heart, a sound that could overwhelm him as it pounded in his ears. He breathed deep. "Just lose yourself," he thought as he studied the vision sprawled out on the sand in front of him, and it was almost as much as his heart could take.

"So beautiful," he thought. "So perfect."

Coach knew this was, in many ways, a waste. He only wanted the one leg from Craig, after all. The left leg, the leg this young man had used so effectively to rocket his body through the hop, the skip then the jump of his record setting triple jumps. Coach admired a committed triple jumper. There was no glory in it, there was no glory in track and field these days, he thought. This age of man had become an age of video games and basement warriors. It was an age of chest thumping and self-aggrandizement. It was an age when even the elite athletes Coach so wanted to admire would strut and preen and beg for praise for having completed the routine.

That wasn't Craig, or rather hadn't been Craig. Young men like Craig took to the discipline out of a love for competition, and an inner drive for success, not praise. Craig had driven himself to perfection despite the lack of adulation. Coach respected that.

"He's a worthy donor," he thought as he wiped down the carrier holding his regulation high school 12-pound shot put and regulation high school discus, just over four pounds. He needed to remove the dripping blood now. It was so much more work to clean if he let it dry and set into the cracks of the vinyl. There was no way avoid any seeping into the fabric, mixing with those who had come before. There was a subtle poetry in that notion, the donors coming together here as they would in his project. Still, practically, it couldn't be so many, nowhere near all 17. He thought, he'd replaced the carrier several times, right? Who knew? A rare statistic he hadn't seen fit to track.

He wiped the carrier almost by rote, pulling his mind back to the beauty unfolding in front of his eyes.

The back of young Craig's head was a concave spiderweb of cuts and rips. The blood was now dripping on the sand. The sand, was it light orange, was it beige? It depended on the light, but it caught the

2

droplets and held them just for a few seconds before absorbing. The black and brown and green gnats and flies and beetles scurrying across this canvas to feed added texture.

"Frame that and you'd have an artwork worthy of any museum," Coach thought. "Jackson Pollock, this is what he was going for. Pure, raw beauty."

A single tear had been forming in Coach's left eye, he could feel the cool evening breeze tracing it down his cheek as his mind turned briefly from the scene now in front of him to the thought that always haunted him.

"There's so much beauty in this world. My project brings me in touch with so much that must be seen and shared. Yet I go through life alone, lonely, with no one with whom to share all this."

But that was simply the reality of the path Coach had chosen for himself. This was by definition not a world to share. It was a shame. In Coach's mind, it was a tragedy. He sighed a heavy sigh.

"I am a man, defined by passion and what I love, but does that passion condemn me to live a life without the love of another," he wondered. Maybe not for so much longer. After all he had this piece, then needed to find a donor for the women's version, and he was done, at least with the project as imagined.

Would there be more to come? Was there another project into which he could throw himself, that would so consume him? Perhaps.

As the evening sun beat down mercilessly, he reminded himself that beyond art, there were also practical matters that needed attention and needed attention now. He took a last loving look, then headed back to his camper van to get his saw.

Chapter 2

April 29, 9:01 p.m.

The Professor let out a long, tired sigh. The world weighed heavy on his shoulders at times like this. To be honest, the world always weighed heavy on his shoulders. To be the guardian of so much knowledge, so much that modern man risked losing, at his peril.

Standing there, taken in isolation and if the rubber apron was dismissed, the Professor absolutely fit his nickname. Under the apron, his jacket was tweed, with patches on the elbows. It was frayed, a bit, but in the Ivory Tower chic sense of frayed - obviously well-worn but also obviously high quality. His shoes, under the clear plastic bags covering them, were professorial Florsheims. Nice, but not too nice,

4

affordable even for the underpaid. Perfect for one who cares about the way he looks, but doesn't want that to show.

His dark hair, under the shower cap, was a bit too long, and pointedly disheveled. His brown eyes, behind the plastic goggles, exuded compassion, yet gave a hint of his personal burden.

The Professor was responsible for carrying what others toss aside. He was responsible "ab ovo usque ad mala" he muttered, from the beginning to the end. It was clear the burden had been and always would be on him. He was, after all, enlightened, and while it was impossible to believe that this younger generation would produce a mind capable of picking up the torch that in him burned so brightly, this was no excuse for him to slow, or pause, or neglect, his search.

"There is no excuse for failure in my task, though," he thought. "Aut viam inveniam aut faciam. I will find a way, or make one. Surely I will have to make the path by myself..."

The professor looked around the room. Overly cluttered, but not in a good way.

"It's no secret what holds back this next generation," he thought with, well, more sadness than disdain, but certainly some disdain. A map of Middle Earth dominated one wall. Pathetic. He wondered what the young student could have been thinking when he'd hung this version of Munch's Scream, rendered with a yellow comic book character (the character was a buffoon, he lamented, named Homer, another insult to enlightenment).

Yet even these travesties, and even the oversized and prurient posters of Hollywood starlets, were light farce when compared to the obvious waste of time and braincells devoted to the large television monitor mounted in prime position in the room. The television was attached to one of those gaming machines. It was appalling, and it explained the simplistic conclusions young Jimmy Nichols had reached in his award winning and therefore allegedly noteworthy paper on young Abe Lincoln.

Typical, and therefore not worthy of being labeled extraordinary in any way, he thought as he flipped through the paper. There were a few red drops on the pages. The sad consequence of failure for young Jimmy. Could he not understand even the depths of his own work?

The Professor looked at him, again. He wanted to be fair. Was he giving Jimmy a fair exam? The ropes, he noted, were not too tight. The young man could speak at will, or at least had been able to before the sixth cut. He had made an enormous amount of noise. But now, as he used the chalk to mark an eighth incorrect, or at least insufficient, answer, Mr. Nichols had been reduced to little more than whimpering.

Odd. He looked healthy enough. True, he was a bit thin. Aristotle would have chastised him for an obvious avoidance of the physical world. But the Professor had been on his mission for three years now, and his research indicated that a tendency towards the asthenic frame was common to universal among the young scholars.

He wondered if this might not, in part, explain their mental failings, as well. Were not the body and mind wed?

"Young man I know you think this is unnecessary, but the reality of true scholarly endeavor is that it is often painful. When we expose our minds to the world, we are opening ourselves to judgement, and that is often quite painful. It is often even more painful than the physical discomfort you now obsess upon. I assure you of this."

"Please." Jimmy Nichols whispered through tears. "Let me go. I didn't do anything to you. I don't even know you."

"Not true. When we enter the rough and tumble world of scholarship, we are all brothers and sisters. Don't sell yourself short. Now think: Lincoln as you note was no great believer in total equality, perceiving differences between the Caucasoid and Negroid races. By today's standards, his beliefs would have branded him a monster, yet how did he reach his conclusions and does this justify his notion of ending one of the 19th Centuries great moral failings by employing another? Discuss…"

"Please don't cut me again, please don't cut me again…"

Nichols was fading, which was a shame. Frankly, the Professor was prepared to be lenient on this topic. Any thoughtful discussion of the moral quandary of ending slavery but embarking on further colonization would have sufficed. He would have been quite happy with a discussion that got around to the truism that people are products of their environment. Lincoln, who followed Thomas Jefferson in this, did not see the fatal error in proposing resettlement through colonization for former African slaves. You cannot, of course, impose your will on a group of people to absolve yourself of having done just that to another group.

The Professor liked this line of thinking, because it came back fairly quickly to the ethos that guided his mission: Those who forget history are condemned to repeat it. The contradictions between the life and myth of Lincoln always made this fertile soil.

"Perhaps that is why I am so often drawn to Lincoln scholars," the Professor wondered as he waited.

But, of course, he could not wait forever.

It did not appear that young Mr. Nichols would be forgetting history, or failing to learn from it, for much longer. He was failing to make the grade and his time would soon pass. All times must pass, of course. The time allotted Mr. Nichols was merely being modified, and when viewed through the lens of history, modified only a little.

In all ways, the Professor reminded himself, this was a good thing. A single, misguided, mind could do horrible damage. While the Professor considered that he was too modest to insist he was doing God's work with his little tests, the question did arise: If not me, then who?

The world going forward needed only the strongest, most committed minds. Those who would dabble around the fringes, coming across as new thinkers but really nothing of the sort, were more dangerous than helpful.

He could remember when he had learned this lesson. On many nights he still burned with the pain of that moment.

He had not always, he reflected, been the torchbearer for the future. He had always, however, that that possibility within him.

The Professor, or rather Dr. Peter J. van Nibben, now 56, had leapt into the limelight of Academia while still a PhD candidate in European history, with an emphasis on Napoleonic France. He was willing to admit, to himself at least, that this doctoral thesis had been a rather sensational work. He had titled it "The Naked General."

As would be the case with all great works, his was equal parts inspiration and perspiration, with a sprinkling of fate tossed in. That fate, even now 30 years later, made him smile.

He's been surrounded by dullards, hoping to fill in the cracks of history with works on the growth of democracy in a time of an evolving printing press and the lessons behind the concurrent development of calculus in England and Saxony.

Such topics were fine for less fertile minds. "Well conceived," he'd told a fellow candidate at the time. "That is the sort of topic at which you could excel."

But the bar would not be artificially lowered for him. A young van Nibben (not yet a professor) knew he had to answer to history. During a visit to Versailles, which his pathetic parents only barely agreed to properly fund, he was walking through the majestic Hall of Generals and stumbled upon his muse. In the midst of a hall of men captured for posterity full military dress, showing the pomposity of an era that had spiraled out of control, was Gen. Wolfgang von Langenglied, who appeared naked.

Looking at that statue, van Nibben understood that he was looking at the definition of power. He set out to prove his theory by tracking the career of Gen. von Langenglied, but learned only that he had come to France from Prussia, and the Professor reflected that it wasn't difficult to understand why.

Here was a man who demanded to be in the center of the world. Here was a man who could not be defined by an outfit. Here was a man who understood the nature of man, and necessity of strength in intent and character.

Sadly, the Professor had found precious little about his General, until he was sifting through old papers at a non-military archive and stumbled across a series of popular works from the time on Gen. Wolfgang von Langenglied.

"Stupid, petty French peasants," he'd realized. "Refused to even spell his name correctly on his statue."

Here was a man the world had wrongly overlooked, but van Nibben had pledged to right that wrong. The work he'd produced had been a sensation. His naked General was a full-blooded man, and his adventures both military and sexual had been extraordinary. Not only had the academic world had to take a step back and make room for him at the top, a position at Yardton University had been waiting, but they had to watch in envy as his work became, according to no less a source than USA Today, a best selling phenomena. He had wealth and power and respect.

By the age of 30, van Nibben was the Professor, and had accomplished everything he had dreamed would await him in life.

Within three years, he had lost it all. Or rather, it all had been taken from him. It had been young so-called young scholars at Yardton, an arrogant, precocious bunch. Fresh from high school, a small group of students had the audacity to challenge his acclaimed thesis.

It made a certain sort of symmetrical sense. Because he had soared so high, he was doomed to fall so low. The children began publishing articles in the student newspaper questioning his premise. His General, they noted, actually spelled his name the way it had been spelled on his pedestal. The lack of information on the man had been the result of a lack of accomplishments.

They later alleged that his sources were, in truth, early pornographic texts produced to amuse the Sun King and his court. Gen. Langenglied, they pompously insisted, when translated to English, meant General Long Member.

9

The idiots. The French had no reason to translate his name. It was what it was. No case he had made in his defense had worked. In an odd twist, his work had briefly increased in sales, before major retailers declared it a work of pornography and banned it from their shelves.

It had been a moment of rebirth for The Professor. His experience had taught him the danger posed to a serious world of young, directionless, and undisciplined, minds. While stripped of his positions and credentials and shunned by his beloved academic world, he understood where the blame truly fell.

If mere children could take down even one as admirable as himself, they must be dealt with, to protect society. He would live out his life without need, his mind and his muse had made sure of that. But he would not be idle. He would protect the world from pretenders such as those who had attacked him, and destroyed a fine and promising career.

The Professor's mind drifted back to Jimmy Nichols' room. Nichols continued to burble and plead, but it was clear no answer was coming. He unscrewed the top of his cane and drew out the long, thin blade usually hidden within. Looking at the blade, he realized he had left a few specks of blood after an earlier question, so he lovingly wiped it clean.

He placed his feet shoulder width apart, and extended the hand holding the blade to young Mr. Nichols head.

"He is fading," he thought. "I suspect this ninth reminder should be a serious one."

The Professor flicked his wrist and blood seeped in weak pulses from Nichols jugular. Nichols was reeling around losing consciousness.

"It is a shame, his lessons were not well learned," he thought.

"Mr. Nichols," he said. "A final question, I think, dealing with the interpretation of history, dealing with Gen. von Langenglied…"

"The Naked General?" Nichols wheezed, almost managing a laugh with one of his last breaths. "You're that frau..."

A second later, the Professor pulled his blade back from Nichols throat for a final time.

"Never interrupt when your Professor is speaking," he said as he again cleaned the blade.

Chapter 3

May 18 9:28 p.m (10 years earlier)

The mirror didn't lie. It couldn't, really. It wasn't some macho asshole who would leave you for, well, whatever that was he had left for, after insisting: "We're doing great, really honey…"

It wasn't filled with self-delusion, or doubt. It wouldn't adapt to suit her mood, it wouldn't offer her comfort on a bad day.

A mirror's reflection was just the truth. As Chrissy Kristens looked into the door sized rectangle, she realized that was both a gift and a curse. She pursed her lips and thought. She used to have such a sexy pout, but that was over. The twisted edge of her mouth, the small spiderweb of ridges the stitches had left behind on her right sided cheek, sadly removed any thought of sexy or cute or beautiful, and pushed her into the unloved and unlovable and overused and rejected category. People would try to tell her otherwise, but people lied.

She made a sad clucking sound, then did a half turn and raised her left leg. Always best to view the calf in Fuck-Me Pumps. She knew this, but they weren't always practical, and certainly hadn't been today. Instead she put her toes on the ground and rested the heel of her flats on the Mom's shoulder. Jo-Anna Erste she'd been called, Chrissy remembered. Putting a little bit of pressure on the heel bunched up her calves perfectly for viewing. Well, as perfect as it got, given the circumstances.

Chrissy had been careful. She'd picked the dry side of the body, avoiding the splatter. The other shoulder was in a pool of muck, and that would not do at all for getting a good, honest look. Not that it helped much. The lacework of scars on her left calf, they could have done with a bit of self-delusion to soften their impact.

"It's too bad," she thought. "It's tragic, really. Admit it, hideous. It's just awful."

Since she was already in a half turn, she couldn't help but to check out her ass. That made her smile. It was still a good ass. She could still bring wolf whistles. Well, if she was wearing long pants, and the whistlers only saw her from behind, and couldn't see the scars covering her leg or cheek. Her ass was not why she was forced to live a lonely life.

As she stepped over the Mom to head back to the others, that thought made her tear up. Here she was, a woman with so much to give, so much to offer, and who once had had it all. God, she had been hot in her day. Sizzling, really.

And now? Now she was more along the lines of burnt. But enough with lamenting the sad death of her love life, or rather her inability to find true love in this life. This day wasn't about her. This day was about saving young Debby. Beautiful, perky, wonderful Debby.

"Debby should not, will not, have to endure, what I suffered through," she thought. "At the very least, I can know I gave her this one gift."

Chrissy admitted that at the same time, Debby represented a big step for her, as well. A turning point in a life that had become not only solitary, but rudderless. Chrissy knew she had been drifting for a while now.

It hadn't hurt her at work. Chrissy remained a top saleswoman. It wasn't a difficult job for her. Cleaning products, after all, were part of the fabric of life. Everyone needed them. Chrissy supposed her deformities didn't hurt in her sales record, either. Never underestimate the power of pity.

But it was after her first afternoon of sales calls in this place, Blue Springs, Missouri, as she'd sat in a Denny's and wondered what life could possibly hold for her beyond 10 crates of the Lemon scented "Grime Buster Extra" and a recurring 10 crates a month of the ammonia based, and floral scented "Pure Clean Super" (which represented the sort of afternoon that kept the bonuses coming) when she'd picked up a discarded local newspaper and found Debby. It had been Debby's smile, shining through even in a black and white photo, and the glitter of a tiara that had caught Chrissy's attention.

"Local girl wins Miss Teen Missouri" read the headline. The article continued, noting that "After wowing judges and an audience by walking a runway in a shimmering evening gown, local girl Deborah Erste walked away with the Miss Teen Missouri title last Saturday. In doing so, she became the first local winner of the state's most prestigious pageant in more than 15 years and made it clear that her future, like her smile, would be charmed."

Chrissy had read the piece, and after a brief pang of jealously had been replaced by a wave of déjà vu, she had realized what this

14

seemingly random article was saying to her. It was time to stop living her life only lamenting her own sad fate. Her story, as tragic as it was, was hardly unique.

It was the way of the natural world. Young beautiful girls grew into old ugly women. True, in her case, a car accident had accelerated the process, but every young beautiful girl would have some form of Chrissy's car accident to deal with. At the very least, it would simply be aging. Their perfect skin would wrinkle. Their perfect breasts would sag. Their perfect smiles would stain and lose that twinkle.

Chrissy teared up whenever she imagined this happening to others like hers. She envied normal girls, those whose beauty never stopped traffic. They had no idea what they were missing, so how could they miss it? How could they understand the pain of this loss.

But Chrissy had lived through it, and she knew it was as intense a pain as any form of torture. With water-boarding, there's at least the hope that you might simply drown. Chrissy's pain, well, there was no end in sight or imaginable. She'd made up her mind in that moment that someone had to do something to help these girls. "If it has to be somebody, shouldn't it be me?" she thought. She had decided it should be. And so, here she was, on the day her own downward spiral had begun, the day on which she had peaked, and after which everything in life was downhill, in Debby's house.

Chrissy knew that the pain she had lived with was what awaited young Debby, young, beautiful Debby. She lifted her large bag onto her shoulders as she stepped around the body of the father in the hallway. She peaked into the bedroom. Spotless. She'd planned well for this. She admitted some of that meticulous planning was really little more than luck.

For instance, she hadn't really given the parents much thought at first. Her mind had been set on saving Debby. She knew what that had to entail. She couldn't destroy the face, that would defeat much of the point of act of kindness. She knew from the first second the thoughts coalesced in her mind that she needed to leave Debby's face the way it had been shining out of that newspaper photo. Perfect.

15

The parents, however, about them she had no such remorse. Chrissy, after all, was only here because they clearly didn't love their daughter enough to do what needed to be done. She wanted to believe it had been a flash of inspiration that had taken her to Big Bob's Gun and Ammo Emporium along Interstate 70 in Missouri. But really it had only been a need to pee, and an otherwise empty stretch of road. Still, the minute she'd seen the 9mm, in a pink camouflage and complete with a matching silencer, she'd had to have it.

At first, she'd been disappointed that the ammo hadn't matched, but thinking through her mission she realized it was actually a good thing. Pink camo ammo would have been a really easy clue for police, and she didn't really want that. Not now that she'd come up with a mission, one that made living through all of this pain worthwhile, despite the loneliness, despite the continuing decay. Copper was fine, in the end. Copper, Chrissy believed, was as much as these people deserved.

Debby deserved more, though. In the end, it had worked out as well as Chrissy could hope. The father had opened the door, and she'd shot him through the forehead and again through the heart before he could consider closing the front door. She followed him as he stumbled backwards, then fell, into the hallway and seen the mother in what looked like a family room. The mother had been sitting in a chair facing the television, her reflection in the wall mirror making it clear she was at least a little lost in her program and hadn't figured out that she would have been best served to have jumped through a window or at least ran away by the time Chrissy was through the doorway. Chrissy's first shot into the left side of the mother's head had taken careful aim, but Chrissy knew the second and third shots were a bit sloppy. She hadn't been able to resist watching herself in the mirror as she pulled the trigger.

She looked good holding a gun on someone, she'd thought. Despite getting sloppy, the first shot had ripped the Mother off the couch and onto the floor, in front of the mirror, luckily. The second and third had only grazed her left side and left shoulder, but they didn't really matter. The first had done the job.

16

Chrissy regretted that the noise of the mother falling in the family room, or the father falling into the hallway, must have alerted Debby to something being amiss. Chrissy had no intention of shooting Debby. She'd instead brought the heavy brass statue she'd been awarded as Miss Teen Garden State. She practiced on watermelons, and was confident a single blow to the back of the head would do the trick. She'd just gripped the statue when Debby ran into the hallway, saw first her father, then her mother, and turned to run as she screamed.

Chrissy had been on her and brought the statue down accurately and with force before Debby had finished yelling the entire word "help." Thinking of it, Chrissy only remembered "hel…" before Debby had dropped.

Chrissy admitted that the excitement of helping Debby had been a bit more of a thrill than she'd anticipated. "I shouldn't be so hard on myself, though," she thought. "I've always been a giving sort of person. Of course, I found helping out like this thrilling."

Dragging Debby down the hallway and into the bathtub had been more difficult than she'd expected, but she'd managed it. Arranging Debby's trophies and photos around the bathroom, in as much of a tribute as she could think of at the moment, had been almost second nature. It really felt like the right thing to do at the time.

Chrissy was ready to leave now. The mission was complete, and had been completed well and without a single problem that Chrissy had not foreseen. That, she thought, was pretty amazing.

Just before heading out, however, she pulled three large candles from her mission bag. Vanilla scented, that was the best, especially as it was a bit hot and humid in this part of the country, and it might be days or even weeks before anyone found Debby and her parents.

She made one last check to ensure the photos were lined up perfectly. She wanted them to be looking down on Debby, and Debby to be looking up at them. Then she lit the candles, and left the house with a bounce in her step.

"This was good," she thought. It had now been exactly 15 years since her life had peaked, which meant 15 years since she had started her descent, and really, this was the first wholly positive experience she'd had. She had no memory of feeling this alive, this energized, since the tiara was placed upon her head 15 years before.

She'd also been 19 back then. Just like Debby. She hadn't thought the world held anything but splendor and joy. Just as Debby clearly believed today. That day, she reflected, would have been the perfect day to die. Debby was a very lucky young lady.

"There are others," Chrissy knew. In her lonely life, with nothing but work and time, she had time to find others. She had time to plan. She had time to kill.

"It's really nice to be needed again," she thought. "Even if Debby didn't know she needed me, she did. She's my girl. Just like those who will follow, all my girls will need a little help. It feels good knowing that I will be there for them."

Chapter 4

April 15th 3:45 p.m.

The soccer ball was behind her, which was annoying because Nev Sparrow had just made a really nice run of 50 yards from her spot as a left back up into the attacking half of the field. Had the pass been perfect, she had nothing but empty grass, a girl in bright orange whose eyes got really big when she noticed Nev's run and space, and some netting between her and the Colorado State Soccer Championship.

Ten minutes left and the game was locked at 1-1. In her mind, Nev knew what a perfect pass would have meant. No defender had tracked her run, at least nobody who could keep up. That's what sneaking up from the defense into the offense meant, the other team often forgot about her.

Nev waited for moments like these. She had the lungs for these moments, too. The girls she had left behind, the 80 minutes of racing up and down the field with or after Nev had left them needing a break. Nev didn't want a break, and she didn't want them to have a break. This had been glory time. Damn.

"Get on your horse, girl," she thought as she dug her Pumas into the grass and cut to her left towards the sideline, and about five yards back. Okay, the player who Nev had stripped of the ball way back near her own goal had made the lung-busting run back onto defense, chasing Nev. She was only a few seconds behind. She had to be dealt with.

Nev reached the ball just before it rolled out of bounds. "Never stop running until the ball is all the way out of bounds," she thought, and smiled. That was her motto. Run all the way through the line every time, chase every lost hope, and sometimes, you get there in time and hope isn't lost after all. Do that twice a game, and that's two possessions you've kept alive that would have ended. Twice in a game might not seem like a lot, but the margin between loser and winner wasn't very wide, most times. In any case, it felt great when she got there in time.

She cradled the ball with the instep of her right shoe, caressed it with the cleats to take the speed down and make it dance back with her as she swerved away from the sideline in a loop back a few steps towards the center of the field. The chasing girl was there now, so she used the bottom of her shoe to step on the ball, lightly, and pull it back under her. Nev came to a complete stop as the girl tried to swing her leg at the ball while still moving as fast as she could run.

As the girl flashed as she tumbled clumsily to the ground, Nev rolled the ball forward, then cut sharply, down the path the girl had been following, before she'd reached for the ball and lost her balance and fallen. With her right foot on the ball, she was past the girl and had pushed the ball downfield before anyone had a chance to react.

Three steps and she was nearing her full speed.

"This is life," she thought. "The sun is shining. The wind in my face. My legs have some strength left, and that move just sent that girl onto her ass."

Nev laughed and took one last dribble with her right foot, pushing the ball out in front of her just far enough that she could take a final stride and cock back her left leg and let this sucker fly.

"This," Nev thought, "is fun."

The goalkeeper was looking wide-eyed again, and the other defenders were scrambling over to stop her from getting her left foot on the ball. They'd been warned about this before the game, every day at practice for a week they'd been warned. Nev was the best soccer player in Colorado high schools. She was always a menace. She played deep, as a defender, and rampaged forward when she saw the chance. But as dangerous as she was at all times and in all areas of the field, the opposing coach had drilled into her girls one overriding warning.

"Do not let her get the stupid ball onto her left foot when it matters," she'd said. "Crazy stuff happens when she has the time to set up that stupid foot. Drive her to the right. Drive her inside. Just don't let her do that voodoo crap she does with her left foot."

But it was too late to act on the warnings, because Nev was at full speed and looking to her right she could feel that the goalkeeper had taken at least a full step too much out towards her, and was cheating towards the goalpost closest to Nev, where Nev had initially thought to curl a shot as hard as she could strike the ball.

But... well, Nev knew as much about the other team as they knew about her, and this goalkeeper wasn't bad, at all. In fact, if Nev wasn't the best player in Colorado, she probably was. So Nev took just a little pace off her foot as it slashed downwards, and hit the ball just a smidge lower and more centrally than she'd first thought she might.

The ball left her foot, arcing up, almost floating, hardly spinning. It went over the goalkeeper's outstretched gloved fingers. The ball reached the top of its arc above the keeper, then started dropping back towards earth. In the end, it hit the inside of the goalpost on the far side of the goal, about a foot from the top, and bounced into the net. Goal.

Of course, now came the celebration part. Nev didn't celebrate, not much. Being honest, she didn't celebrate well.

"Come on, there are still nine minutes of game left," she rationalized. But she knew the truth was she was horrible at the celebration. She tried. She really did try. But as Sophia, who'd made the pass, even if it was a step behind, would note, Nev always looked like a goof when she tried to celebrate. She stretched out her arms and wooped and ran towards the corner flag and realized she looked just like a little kid playing airplane. She tried to hide this in a quick turn and, bonk, head first right into Sophia, who'd come running to jump into her arms and hug and celebrate, and was now on her back holding her head, but laughing.

"Wow, you are bad at this, aren't you."

"Sorry."

"Hey, you scored."

Nev offered a hand and lifted Sophia back to her feet, as the others arrived, also laughing. "Worst one yet, impressive," someone said.

So true, Nev thought. "Well, back to work, I guess," she said.

The newspaper reporter from the Denver Post who had been covering the state final, however, didn't laugh and didn't need to see much more to know how she was going to start her story. The next day, Nev would blush a little when she saw the Post's website begin the story about the game by writing: "With just minutes remaining in a state championship game, the left foot of Colorado Prep Athlete of the Year Nev Sparrow produced the kind of magic it's been making for three years around the state. The goal, when it finally settled into the net, was part artistry, and part brute force. But it was hardly unexpected, as Sparrow's left leg is as close to perfection as this state has seen in decades.

"Sparrow, who earlier this year received top honors from the White House for her academic performance, and even won the state's highly controversial Miss Teen contest, with this title made a strong case for her place at the top of Colorado athletics.

"While the odds against one 18 year old rising to the top in brains, beauty and brawn in a single year might seem impossible, Sparrow seems to have reached all three summits within the past six months. To say the least, this has been a dream come senior year for the young woman from Chances … "

Chapter 5

May 17th. 9:01 p.m.

"We're probably looking for three psychos, not just one like they thought at first. I did the research and I'm pretty sure, they're pretty sure as well that it's not one guy or even two, but really three..."

"Okay, Bro. Super creepy. I hear that, but exactly why are you telling me this?"

It was, Nev thought, a very fair question. Her brother was of course leading up to the point where he would tell her he wasn't going to make it out of Virginia, to the family home in Chances, Colorado, for the next ten days. He had promised their parents he would be there, and in fact he had promised he would be arriving about right now.

But work had gotten in the way. Work always got in the way of his visits.

Nev didn't care much that her big brother was going to be late, or not make the trip at all. She was, after all, just a couple months from turning 19. She was just weeks separated from the high of winning the state championship in soccer. So her parents had taken their long promised second (and really first) honeymoon just after her high school graduation. So they were in the Maldives by now, in one of those crazy cool cabins built out over turquoise water. So they were pretty much out of contact for two weeks.

She was not a kid, and she didn't need a baby sitter. She was fine on her own. She was more than fine.

"Freakin' great," she'd announced as soon as their car made the turn out of sight at the end of Chances Ave. Sure, it would have been a blast if every single one of her friends hadn't already taken off on family vacations. Even Sophia had taken off, which kind of sucked because, well, they'd been planning on hanging out after graduation and now here Nev was with "a whole freakin' house to herself and no freakin' parents around," (as she'd explained to Sophia), and she was gone, and they all were gone. "It's Hawaii," Sophia had said. Others had tossed in "Grand Canyon" and "the Florida Keys." One had noted "my Grandma is really sick and might be dying so I've gotta go." Okay, that last one she understood.

The rest were plain annoying. Nev was a little bit jealous, honestly, but mostly annoyed. Tromping around canyons, lying on the beach, whatever, it all lost a bit of its shine when every couple of minutes you had deflect questions about "your plans for the future."

So as soon as her parents had vanished from sight ("Maybe that means they don't exist. A bit of solipsism for you Nev," she said inside her head. "Or is that logical positivism? Damn, out of school for a week and already it's all going away.") she'd set about making this house into her home. For two weeks at least, this was Nev's place, and two weeks, well, that was a decent amount of time.

First item of business, unplug the stupid landline phone.

"Has that thing ever been for me, since I was like 10?" The answer was a clear no, but it was gonna ring and ring loudly all day long, or at least in the morning when she wanted to sleep, and these two weeks had a lot to do with sleep. She'd grabbed the handset and walked through the house, dusting (which was on the list, Jeebus, they're off to islands and I'm dusting) and finally dropped it in a random drawer which she had made a point to forget but was probably in the big bureau in the living room. "I mean," she thought, "it definitely is, but I'm forgetting that. This is my time to be irresponsible and lazy and self-centered, and count those all as positives."

So after she'd dumped the landline, she spent four hours working her way through the chore list from Hell ("Stupid Dad with his stupid jokes."). Example: Do a full pool treatment. The filters are all full of that green gunk from the winter. But be careful, it's a strong acid, so wear the gloves, and don't use it around your Mom's ink pots and make another mustard gas!"

Freakin' unbelievable. Once! One school project, and it was years ago, ends with the school being evacuated because you did exactly what you'd set out to prove could be done, which was pretty cool if you really thought about it, and forgot about the woman from Holland who showed up in a moon suit to do the testing and disinfecting. Still, he has to get on me about that.

I haven't done that forever. Could I still even remember how? She ran the formula through her head ($(HOCH_2CH_2)_2S + 2\ HCl \rightarrow (ClCH_2CH_2)_2S + 2\ H_2O$) and smiled. Oh yeah. But I wouldn't. I'm not crazy.

She had also been assigned to pick up her Mom's studio on the top floor, up the creaky winding stair case. Cool room, really. Amazing light. It was above the tops of the trees and almost all glass. It was also the only room in the house where her Mom was now allowed to keep her Big Ol' Pot of Blue. The blue was a bit heavy on the Thiodiethylene glycol. Her mom mixed it herself, and well, when Nev had been obsessed with the chemistry, it hadn't taken her long to figure out that the pool cleaner was almost pure hydrologic acid.

Back then, she'd messed around with it, and eventually came up with her infamous science experiment. And well, there was now a two-floor rule. The two items couldn't be closer than two floors to each other.

Her Dad, wag that he was, had also insisted that because someone in the family might mistakenly think rules are meant to be broken it was smart to install an incredibly cool escape ladder from the bird's nest of a room. It was a rope ladder, and it didn't quite get you all the way down to the ground, but close enough.

Her Dad later admitted it was more of a fire precaution. He didn't want her Mom to get caught up in her perch if something went wrong. Nev and Brody had spent years of their childhood trying to come up with excuses to throw the thing out of the window and climb down the outside of the house. They'd been allowed, once, to see how it worked. Since then, the closest Nev got to it was looking it over for fraying twice a year as part of her spring and fall cleaning chores.

She was remembering this as she was wiping down the outside of her Mom's colors, being careful with the blue, because, well, she'd had problems with that before). That was her approach to the list. Outside first, then from the top down.

The pool was cleaned, or as clean as she was going to get it.

Then her Mom's studio. There really wasn't much to do there. Fasten the lids (they were mostly loose and some were open. Check the windows, all locked. Wonder if she shouldn't try out the ladder, since, who would know, but maybe later.

Then she creaked down the steps to her the second floor. Jeez this is a grossly oversized house. If her Mom and Dad had been here, she'd have spent at least an hour or two complaining about the list. It was massive. Well, it was almost massive. She knew that if she stuck to it, it would be done in a max of two or three hours.

"If I'd had a single friend not abandon me, I'd be really pissed," she thought.

As it was, what else was she going to do?

Still, mostly the list was just a lot of stupid little things.

Sheesh, though, this house is huge. I never want a big house. Give me a cozy apartment. And don't even get me started on having a yard. What is the point? Well, when you're a little kid, the yard is great. But now? I guess if you like mowing and raking leaves…

Her thoughts were interrupted by a voice in her ear. It sounded like Bro. What was he doing on her phone? Oh, right.

"Seriously, Bro, when you do actually get here, should we break out the ladder, give it one last climb?" she blurted out, and he laughed.

"You're not listening at all, are you?"

"I was, for a bit."

"Maybe, we'll see, You should listen to this though, it's really fascinating and …"

But Nev's mind was off again. In her defense, the house was huge. It almost looked like a slasher movie house. That might be a bit much, she thought, but it is huge.

The basement had six rooms, five of which surrounded an idiotic central room. And the rooms all connected with doors, both to the stupid middle room and to the rooms to each side. It was almost like a carnival fun house, or one of those old movies where cops with batons would chase the hero, and the villain, in and out of doors in a central hallway. In those movies, the joke was apparently that the doors through which people were running into the hallway didn't make sense. But with the central room, it made sense. It still wouldn't be funny, but at least it would make sense.

Still, it had been great for hide and seek games in the winter when she was a kid.

Her mom had taken the central room, which was probably actually just a really oddly shaped hallway, and started storing old mirrors, from estate sales or grandma and grandpa, or Granny B's estate, and turned it into their own private house of mirrors. Not that anyone would ever want one of those. There were about 50 mirrors in the thing now. It was crazy.

The mirrors were never used. That room was never used. It had one way too bright light in the ceiling, no chairs, no table, just mirrors and doors. Nev assumed her Mom's "Clean the mirrors" note had to be a joke.

That place was creepy, and her mom had to know she would avoid that room if at all possible, especially being home along. So she'd ignored that part of the list. She had checked to make sure the windows in every stupid room on all three floors were closed, and she'd made sure the shutters were all secured. ("Of course this house would have shutters. Who has shutters?").

I am a hell of a good daughter, she'd thought.

She'd snagged all the cobwebs from the chandeliers in the living room and checked the trash baskets in every room, even her brother's, which hadn't really been his since he moved out years ago. Her aunt had once forgotten to do this after her uncle had died, and a month later she went into his studio and there were flies everywhere. One of his last acts before his heart attack had been to throw away a sandwich in his home office. Nev had no intention of dealing with that sort of crap.

As instructed, she swept and vacuumed forever, or at least for half an hour. She planned on staying in her fuzzy socks, or being barefoot, for the next two weeks, so this was all right.

They'd told her to dust and arrange all the trophies. She was pretty sure this was her Mom and Dad's way to remind her that she'd done well in school. Yeah, I know that, she thought.

The trophies were in the sitting room attached to her bedroom on the second floor. She used it as an exercise room.

She arranged her trophies on the shelves her Dad had built. She pushed each and every Judo and Karate and soccer trophy back from the edge of the shelf. She found the trophies embarrassing. But it was a good kind of embarrassment, when she was alone, at least.

When people were around, it was the bad kind of embarrassed. Kind of braggy. But her Dad had built the shelves, then arranged them that way, and every time a new one came in he added it. She had to admit, she liked the progression of her soccer trophies. The early ones had photos of the teams, and seeing herself in pigtails and a crazy big smile made her happy. The karate and judo trophies were all ancient. She'd stopped going to tournaments at least five years ago.

The newer ones were kind of clunky and big. Miss Teen Colorado was almost terminally bad. The reality was, it wasn't really real. "I mean, how was I to know? Other than paying attention, but in my defense, nobody from Chances had the slightest idea. That was a Denver thing, a Boulder thing. I just went because Mom asked me to enter and I wanted to make her happy. Was that so bad? I had no idea I'd win. I really had no idea why I'd win."

The Presidential Merit plaque didn't really fit with the others, but she was proud of that. She liked how it was next to her 8th grade Oportunidad County Chemistry Contest first place, which made her look well rounded. She also liked how Ms. Blake had taped a note to it saying "And you didn't even kill any of us!" to the trophy. "Take that Dad, stupid joke but I won, didn't I?"

The all-state stuff for soccer, those made her proud.

Then she ran the dishwasher and put everything away. She stuffed all her dirty clothes in the washer and washed, then dried, the lot.

And she was done. Finished. Free.

During the next two weeks, she was going to ignore everything around her. She was going to lay down and relax and not care, at all, about anything.

When she was done with that, finally had everything squared away, she could feel the pressure leave through her head. She went to her computer and called up a list of "What to watch when I have time" and "What to eat when I don't care."

Nev would be just fine on her own.

Nev saw herself as a badass, though she wondered if the fact that she felt she had to complete an entire list of chores before entertaining these bad ass thoughts might not detract from her bad-assesdness. She knew others saw her as the perfect kid. She was pretty. Adults told her she was really pretty. This was more than a bit disgusting.

Nev prided herself on being an unkempt brunette. She had hair that she allowed her mother to cut now and then, but had only once had her hair really styled. She'd learned on cold mornings as she was running for the school bus that if she didn't waste time drying her hair first she'd have an extra seven minutes of sleep, and if she ran a comb through her hair once she'd made the bus, voila, she'd scrape the ice away and have mostly dry hair. Nev took proud in not working on how she looked, with the one exception. She never used makeup, outside of that contest. She dressed in tee-shirts that made her laugh, and baggy hoodies, and jeans. She wore running shoes most of the time, and cleats a good portion of the rest.

She cared about being a good student and she loved playing soccer. She was good at both school and soccer. She liked being the smart kid, and she loved being able to rip open a soccer game.

She'd just finished a senior year during which she'd worked hard and had success, and right now, she really wanted a break, some time to relax by herself.

She didn't need her brother to leave his training at the FBI, especially just as he appeared to be loving it. She was safe and sound in their small town. She'd be fine, even with no friends, even all alone, except for some pizza, some chips and a lot of streaming.

In Chances, the problems of her teenage years weren't so much dealing with too much risk or danger, but finding enough to keep her from falling asleep before midnight.

Bro's voice again cut into her daydream. Man, the guy is 25 and in the FBI and he can drone on forever about random stuff. But he was her brother, and one of her favorite people on Earth, and she knew he'd move heaven and earth for her (which she thought was an odd expression. If you moved both, wouldn't they probably just seem to end up where they started?).

"I'm shadowing Special Agent Paul Carc. He taking me out, my first time in the field. He's attached to the serial killer group, the Behavioral Analysis Unit right now. The ones on that show you love to get creeped out by. So he takes me on this case. Unreal. It's this kid, really smart kid, kid who's won all kinds of smart kid awards even like that Presidential Merit deal..."

"Like me."

"What? Yeah, I suppose. In any case..."

"Really creepy, Bro."

"Sorry, but really, this was in Maryland, like 2,000 miles away. Anyway, my guy got called in to consult and took me along. You know I've been at crime scenes before, but this one is weird. Really structured. Usually murder is messy and violent, this time the victim is a kid, 17, and he's tied into a wooden chair. He's been stabbed to death, but not all at once, not a brutal hack like in a fight, the way the other murders I've seen looked. This is more precise. He's been flicked to death, like with a crazy sharp, thin blade. My guy wonders if it wasn't a rapier blade..."

"Great. This is fun."

"Not fun, really, but yeah, kind of..."

"Asshole."

"The room is totally tidy. It was the kid's room. Jimmy Nichols, but we're pretty sure the killer picked up the place. Nothing out of place, except there are these chalk marks on the wall, divided like a scorecard, with a line down the middle. And on the one side there are four marks, but the other, there are 10. And I wasn't thinking anything about it, there was way too much else to focus on, but my guy is talking with the forensics people and there are 10 cuts in Nichols' shoulder, neck and head. That's how he died, same number of cuts as marks on the wall."

"So he was cut 10 times…"

"Well, 11 times, but one was in his leg. Behind his knee, and that matches the blood we found in the kitchen. We think that was where he was standing when the killer somehow cut his leg and disabled him."

"We?"

"Well, my guy, but it's weird isn't it?"

"What do the marks mean? The killer was keeping score?"

"Yeah, something like that."

"Of what?"

"We don't know that. But it was interesting enough that I was sent back to the office to do some research in the national crime database on similar murders, similar victims."

"Both geeky and gross."

"I found a bunch of cases. Way more teens are murdered than you'd think. Most of them are solved. I mean, usually it's the parents or their friends, or, you know, a school shooting…"

Nev started to drift away. She could have told her mom and dad that Bro would be late. Bro was always late. He'd always been late. She knew there would be no catching up with big brother tonight.

She thought a bit and amended: Well, he's always late ish.

She had to admit that when she'd really needed a big brother, he'd been there. When Jordan had been picking on her in fifth grade … well, bad example, because while Bro had finally had words with Jordan, it was after she'd decked Jordan with a well-placed elbow

33

during a recess soccer game. The memory made her laugh, though she thought that was only in her mind.

"Why are you giggling? This really isn't giggly stuff here…"

"Yeah, sorry. So you found your killer?"

"What, no. I found 27 other cases that seemed pretty similar. But when you study the photos, seven of them were almost identical. The others had similar victims, but they were really different. The first group was really smart kids."

"Yeah, wonderful, like me. Noted."

"The second group was bigger, more like 13 kids. They were all really successful high school athletes…"

"Come on, Bro. You know I was all state in soccer. Now you're just trying to creep me out."

"Ha, yeah, true. And the third group was beauty queens."

"Thank god I dodged that one."

"Hey, you were Miss Teen Colorado."

"Kind of."

"You were."

"By default."

It was Bro's turn to laugh.

"Listen jerk, Mom made me enter. I had no idea what was going on."

"I know, I know. It's just funny. Still, you were a beauty queen. It is pretty much the title of the thing."

"Perfect. Just great. I'm serial killer bait."

"Yeah," he said, still chuckling.

"Should I be worried?"
"What? God, no."

"But you're telling me…"

"Get real, Nev. This is a big country. More than 300 million people live here. There are 50 states and you live in one of thousands of small towns. This isn't about you, the odds are a million to one, probably several million to one, that you're safe. You're in far more danger when you drive to the store, or step out of the tub. We've talked about this before. The chances that these psychos would ever come within a hundred miles of you are astronomical."

"I do live in Chances, Bro."

"Ha, good point."

"Anyway, you're about to catch them, right."

"I wish, Sis. I mean, right now we barely know a thing about them."

Nev sighed. She wasn't going to actually get upset about some random psychos from half a world away. She knew that. She also didn't much care that she was being left alone for now, at least, because Bro was busy. But it was fun messing with him.

"So, when are you getting here?"

"Nev, I'm going through the files. I'm trying to identify patterns, if there are any. I wish I could be there. Sorry sis, I'm gonna to be late. Not tonight, obviously. Maybe not tomorrow. The next day, probably. Is that okay?"

"Late? What are the odds on that?" But Nev was smiling as she said it. "I will try to survive without you."

She was actually thrilled. Relaxing with Netflix and junk food, with the remote, the couch, the house and couch all to herself. Could life get any better?

"I think maybe I can catch the red eye tomorrow, be there when you wake up in two days. You're okay until then?"

"Bro, it's one day. What can happen?"

Chapter 6

May 11th 9:22 a.m.

Special Agent Brody Sparrow was the new guy, so he knew he got the crappy chair. He was okay with the crappy chair. It was, after all, a chair. It wasn't as if they made him sit on a bouncy chicken as some sort of a prank. He just got the chair that didn't have top end lumbar support. He figured he was years away from caring about lumbar support.

He got the crappy office, or actually a cubicle in the crappy office. He didn't get much natural light, unless fluorescent lights were natural. Natural light didn't make it into the basement. His desk was old and the drawers only worked if he used excessive force. He supposed it made sense, because in the end he also got the crappy cases, or more accurately the crappy work that went into building the good cases.

But he had access to the same data that was given to agents 40 years his senior. And when he made requests, they carried the same authority of the same FBI. And even the crappy bits of these cases were still important cases, and could make a difference and strike blows for a civilized society and all that, so, when he been asked by his supervising agent Carc to determine how many cases there were that might be similar to the horrors they'd seen in Maryland, he jumped to it.

Agent Sparrow imagined that decades earlier, the results would have been delivered in manila folders and consisted of pages of carbon triplicate copies, or even later when he'd have been handed sheaves of continuous feed ink-jet printouts, the pages still connected and hemmed by the removeable tracks that lines led the paper through the printers.

Here, the search results returned him just as a list on a computer screen. He felt he was losing points for cool in this. The advantage he had was speed. His only real problem had been coming up with the right search terms to feed into the National Crime Information Center, or NCIC. He'd given it a few tries that returned thousands of cases, then he tried:

Dates: Within last 20 years.

Victims: Older than 14, younger than 22.

Case Status: Open. Unsolved, foul play suspected.

Victim Status: Dead or Missing/Presumed Dead.

Race: No filter.

Region/State/City: All.

Suspects: None.

He wasn't searching FBI files, as the most of these cases wouldn't have come to the FBI, or if they had they'd have come to the FBI after starting with local cops. Murder cases, after all, were state crimes, and state crimes were investigated by police departments and sheriff's departments.

He'd struggled for a while, before realizing that all he really had to do was take a couple pieces of the info Maryland police had filed on his last case, and turn that into a wide-ranging search. Adding in the Missing element was his brainstorm. Never know, and he couldn't imagine it would add much in terms of actual numbers.

"This," he thought, "is almost the definition of a tight group."

Hit enter and well, this was almost too fast, too easy, he was thinking when the cases popped up on his screen.

"Two-hundred and eighteen?" he said aloud. "How the fuck is it possible that there are 218 cases that meet these search criteria?"

He thought about it for a few minutes. Really, in the end, his search was just about dead kids. That's too broad, but keep it narrow?

"Parents," he thought. "Most kids were killed by their parents. But parents wouldn't have anything to do with these."

So he removed parents/family from the suspects entry and the list came back at 122. He shortened the time period to 10 years, figuring, well, 10 years is a long time for a killer to wander free, and that knocked the number of possibly similar cases to 84.

"Crap," he realized. Eighty-four was a lot, but it was no where near too many cases to comb through, one at a time. The list he'd called up linked to case files in most cases. In others, the older ones, it simply listed the case numbers. He'd have to look at the details of each case, which would take some time.

"What the hell else do I have to do, though," he thought. True, he'd promised to show up and babysit his little sister in a week, but she was 18 and he had a whole week. He could get through the cases by then, surely.

He went through the list and culled all the cases that didn't link to case files, and then spent the rest of the morning sending out requests for electronic copies of those files. If the cases fit into whatever narrative he was building, he'd have time to get the actual files later.

That accounted for 17 cases. Good, not done, not even really started, but delayed. All he had to worry about right now were the 67 cases he had left. He clicked on the first, from almost exactly 10 years ago.

Date: May 18

Location: Blue Springs, Mo.

Victim (s): Deborah Erste, 19. Jo-Anna Erste, 44. Johnathon Erste, 45.

Okay, he thought. Starting out with a triple.

Cause of death (s): D. Erste, daughter of other two victims, was killed by repeated blows from a blunt instrument to the back of her head. Victim was found in bathroom tub. Appears to have been murdered in her bedroom. Photos of victim were arranged around her body in tub, as were various trophies (Miss Teen Missouri, Miss Sorghum, Miss Jacomo). Two candles were burning, decreasing odor. It appears almost certain that killer suffered remorse at this murder.

Jo-Anna and Jonathon Erste (parents) were found shot to death. Father shot in face and chest. Mother shot in back of head and chest. Appears to follow military doctrine (One in the heart, one in the head). Both appeared to die from head shots, though chest shots also could have been fatal. Parents were left where shot. She was found on floor in living room. He was found in kitchen in front of open refrigerator door.

Suspects: None identified.

Working theory: Father was target of murder, perhaps organized crime related, as shot to face is known to be a message killing. The murders came during a power struggle in area upon the death of longtime regional mob boss Jimmy "Weasel" Mastro. The theory became mother and daughter were collateral damage, but professional killer hadn't expected daughter to be home and was bothered by younger woman's murder. Staged a memorial to assuage his guilt? No sexual molestation, pre or post, was found, which seemed to confirm theory.

Primary Evidence: Bullets standard 9mm, no previous. Site was professionally cleaned. No prints, no DNA. Blunt instrument might have been a ball-peen hammer or something similar.

Case status: Open.

Agent Sparrow looked at the case examination notes. There was a flurry of activity in the months after the murders were discovered. But there hadn't been much at all to add for the past 8 years. One detective's note from just last year, however, mentioned attempt to find a link between this killing and the death of a young woman in Eau Claire, Wisconsin. Victim's were displayed in similar fashions, but in Eau Claire case parents were unharmed, so the matter was determined to be "interesting but unrelated" and the note concluded, "deemed to be yet another dead end. Organized crime angle still makes most sense."

"Not cold so much as freezing," Agent Sparrow thought. Still, it was worth placing on a "further review pile" he was planning on keeping.

Still, as he went through the cases something jumped out at him, a date: May 18. The dates of the other murders looked to be a jumble of random. But May 18, that showed up nine times, every year for the past nine.

"Holy crap, that's in a week," he thought. In fact, it was a day he's scheduled to be off work, back in Chances with Nev while their parents were gone on a second honeymoon. "Taking off is a bad idea," he thought. "I need to be here, just in case I'm on to something. In any case, the last place I need to be is hanging out with my sister."

Chapter 7

May 18, 1:38 p.m.

Brody Sparrow was so deep in thought that when he finally raised his head, he was surprised to find that he was now alone in the office. Late lunches, on site work, or taking off early for long weekends, could have been any of those and probably all of them. He'd been buried in the records and would be for hours. The internal struggle going on inside his head intensified when he realized there weren't any witnesses around to see him give in and head out.

Patterns were emerging. Agent Sparrow didn't like where they were heading.

41

"Maybe I'm just overtired," he thought.

Agent Sparrow looked the part of the young man just breaking in at the Bureau. He was the right height, a smidge over 5'9". He was muscular, but trim. His shoulders were broad enough to indicate that he had been a high school football player, but his size said he hadn't quite had what it would take at the college level.

His suit was a basic blue, off the rack.

In truth, it was one of three identical ones he owned, but he wore in rotation, dry cleaned once every two weeks. It was enough, for now. But he had his eyes on the sales. It would do him no good to wear a cheap suit. There was no point in that. Instead, he waited for sales when he could get something decent enough for $200 or so.

So, for now, his three-suit rotation was enough. Unless he'd had a lunch accident, which he had, uhm, not today, was it yesterday? He hadn't been home to change, at least he knew that. Never get the marinara sauce, even if it was take-out from Carmines. He knew this, yet he continued to break this fundamental rule. He liked the marinara sauce at Carmines.

But he couldn't waste time now thinking about the stain on his tie. And his jacket. And his right leg. He was on to something.

When he'd headed back from the crime scene just outside of Silver Spring a couple weeks back (he checked his notes, May 3rd), he'd been looking for anything, really. His guy, Agent Carc, had given him time and space to work. Carc hadn't been too impressed with what he'd turned up to this point, but told him to keep digging. He'd liked the May 18 finding, but noted it had looked to have fuck and all to do with Silver Spring.

It hadn't been until shortly before he'd talked with Nev that he'd really seen the patterns emerge, and telling Nev about it had actually helped him get his thoughts in order. Three killers, all operating in the same general space. Each with their own subset and methods.

He was pretty sure, at least. The first group, which was first because it was the one he'd set out to find, looked like it had 8 victims. The victims were all smart kids. They were killed in a meticulous, consistent fashion. These were not murders committed as acts of rage. But there was an obvious burning rage underlying the murders.

The victims, all between 16 and 20, were tortured. They died slowly. They died drip by drip. They died knowing they were dying, over an hour, or hours.

That meant someone was with them watching them die. That someone knew enough to edge them slowly and surely towards death, but kept them alive. That also implied that someone enjoyed the ride. He could only imagine what the marks on the wall meant, and none of the things he could imagine were nice.

So the killer was smart. The killer was filled with rage, and it was rage directed at the victims. The killer was calm. The killer was sadistic. The killer was methodical.

The killer's methods were also significantly different than those responsible for the other victim sets. One set wasn't technically murders. Only two bodies hadn't been found, but he'd lumped 13 into the group. In addition to the two who had been found, another 11 high school athletes had vanished in the last 15 years. The additional cases popped up in his research because the missing were listed as "presumed dead, foul play suspected." Agent Sparrow felt it had to mean something. If it did, it meant something bad. Taken as a group, seven boys, six girls had been killed or vanished, after attracting attention for their athletic prowess. The victims ran cross country, took part in track and field, played baseball and softball, boys and girls basketball, football, volleyball, boys and girls tennis, boys soccer.

The two victims who had been found had been mangled. A boy and girl, both found with a missing arm (he, a discus thrower from Maine, was minus a left arm. She, a tennis player from Idaho, was missing her right arm.

Beyond that, they'd been savagely beaten. The coroners in both cases had been at a loss to explain what they'd been beaten with. Some sort of blunt object that had a round head and a straight edge, right next to each other. Looking closely at the photos, the blunt pieces of this blunt instrument appeared to be adjustable. The injuries were consistent, a round indentation and a straight edge, same size each time, but sometimes close together, sometimes a bit spread apart.

"What the hell is going on with this," he wondered.

There was more data to study on the third subset he'd identified. The May 18 group.

This one included a slightly tighter group, all young women, who were killed at 18 or 19. The murders hadn't been tied because as in the first case, their parents, or a parent, often died in the attacks. The investigations had all focused on the parents as the targets. They'd all been shot. The young women were all seen as collateral damage, regret killings. Their bodies were treated with honor.

But what if that was backwards? Agent Sparrow was actually fairly certain at this point the investigations had looked at the killings from the wrong angle.

Each murder included victims who had been beauty pageant winners, at least of some sort. That hadn't been obvious at first from the records, but when he started looking for it, it was there. One was a former Iowa Pork Queen, whatever that was. There were nine girls in total, though the number of murders rose to 17 in this subset counting parents.

The parents came from all over the spectrum. Two parent families, single parent. The parents did not appear to be targets, however. They all died from a 9mm gunshot wound to the head. They were left where they fell. It was one of the things that made it clear those murders were different from the other subsets.

It was the young women who sealed that opinion. While at first glance they could appear to be part of a single, larger group of victims with the other sets, these young women almost universally were not smart and were not athletic. From what Agent Swallow could see, there was no overlap of the other groups into this one, either.

These victims died very different deaths from the other subsets, and from their parents. These victims were attacked, violently, from behind. They all showed severe wounds to the back of their heads.

The reports made it clear that these wounds sometimes killed the victim, sometimes left them unconscious, but that there was no torture going on. This was a swift, single blow and appeared to be intended to incapacitate the victims, permanently. The forensic studies of the bodies didn't indicate that the victims ever awoke from the initial attack. Those who lived through the attack were beaten repeatedly in the face until dead. Those who died during the initial attack were beaten in the face after death.

This killer showed rage directed at his victims, but also showed a bizarre compassion. The crime scenes, aside from the grizzly corpses, were cleaned. Not wiped for prints cleaned, or to remove evidence clean, but seriously cleaned, as if cleaned by someone who really knew his way around cleaners. The cleaning went beyond blood.

The bodies were all found in the victim's bathtub. But if the killings followed a struggle, there was no sign of that, in any of them. Parents in each case would note that their daughter's room had never looked as tidy as it did when they discovered her body.

In each case, photos and trophies, all the accomplishments of a young life, appeared to have been arranged for viewing. The bodies, meanwhile, were covered by quilts. The setups looked to take attention away from the victim, and lead the eye to the photos and trophies. They were almost homages.

"What the hell is going on there," he said aloud, though only to himself.

The last attack had been in Eau Claire, Wisconsin. Like clockwork, exactly one year before there had been a murder in Newark, New Jersey.

Chapter 8

May 18th, 8:56 p.m. (one year earlier)

"It's a shame when they have such nice carpet," Chrissy Kristen thought as she studied her ninth attempt to make the world a better place.

Chrissy Kristen, after all, did not like leaving a mess. It simply was not polite. It was rude, in fact.

Because of this, Chrissy had worked hard since that first day in Missouri so long ago to get better and better at what she needed to do. How much better she'd become always made her smile.

"It's nice to do good," she thought. "In the end, doing so much good is almost selfish. It makes me feel so much better about myself that at times it's hard to remember that this is really all about my girls."

Back in the beginning, with Debby, the plan had worked, but she hadn't been entirely convinced it would work. Today? Chrissy had no doubts. Her methods had been honed and refined through the years. She was always learning, always pushing herself to be a better Chrissy. Each day she'd force herself to look herself square in the mirror and repeat "Win, win, win." The stakes were high. The girls were in need.

And she had gotten much more efficient.

Take today, for example, she thought.

Chrissy was not here to create headaches and heartaches. She knew that in the short term, these would come. But in the long term? She believed in the long term she was acting in the best interests of everyone and most especially, the girls. Pretty young Carol Rose was better off now. Chrissy had protected her. She was here to help.

She flipped open a shiny red notebook with a 3-D heart seeming to hover above the cover. By now she knew how to flip open to the exact page she was looking for. She visited it quite often, whenever the girls had carpet. Could she do it by memory by now? Probably, but why take a chance. If it was worth doing it was worth doing perfectly.

She looked down at the floral swirls of the red ink (color coding counts), and smiled. Her handwriting really was pretty.

"Try pretreating bloodstains with WD-40. But quickly, no dawdling and letting the blood set. Use a very lightly damp sponge to soak up excess liquid. Then spray.

"Wait three minutes before scrubbing. Use the good brush, but remember to rinse it quickly.

"Allow to dry while mixing a cornstarch paste (2 parts cold water to 1 part cornstarch).

"Apply the paste, wait for a couple minutes, then scrub off. Use a clean brush.

"Hoover up the remaining particles.

"IMPORTANT: Turn off lights and shine Game tracker UV light on area. If it shows clean, we're done. If not, repeat. And no shortcuts!"

Just in case, she flipped back to the previous page.

"Remember to get the plastic tarp down ASAP" was in big letters she'd traced over three times, to highlight their importance.

She'd done that, of course. But it was highlighted because it was so important. She pushed and pulled and moved Carol a bit closer to the center. Then she wrapped the tarp tight and lifted Carol off the ground. Chrissy was amazingly strong for her petite frame. She had not started this way. She remembered having to drag girls through their hallways to the bath. That was undignified, and a bit impolite.

She was much stronger now. She realized she could get stronger without too much ruining her figure. and carried her to the bath, carefully stepping around the Mom.

Looking down she muttered, "If you'd just loved her more, I wouldn't have to be here."

As usual, she had nothing but disdain for the Mom. She deserved the single shot to the head Carol had fired into her face. The pink Colt 9mm pistol continued to fulfill its important role. She had no need to waste time on parents who clearly were failing her girls. This one had opened the door and before she'd finished asking Chrissy what she wanted, Chrissy had shoved the gun in her face and pulled the trigger.

"Stupid bitch," she thought as she looked down on the wreck of a woman.

Chrissy loved Carol, though. So much. She loved all her girls.

She set Carol down in the tub. Carol wasn't moving, but maybe she was still breathing? There was a little condensation on the inside of the plastic tarp.

"You sleep sweetie. I'll be right back."

She left the bathroom. She sprayed the WD-40. Then, as the WD-40 worked on the stains, she picked up her work bag and returned to the bathroom.

She opened the bag and dug down into the bottom. A few seconds later she was holding her prized Miss New Jersey 1996 statue. It was beautiful, a shining stainless-steel statuette. It always reminded her of a shapely version of an Oscar. She got nostalgic every time she held it.

It came to her, after all, at the highpoint of her life. She remembered standing on that stage, the lights. Cameras flashing. All eyes were on her. All eyes were always on her in those days. When she walked down the hall in school, boys turned their heads to follow her. On the street, men whistled and propositioned her several times every day. Other girls would tell her it was demeaning and sexist and on and on, but she knew they were jealous.

Being pretty and perky and young meant free coffee when the male baristas or clerks were working. It meant her favorite shops remembered her name, and her measurements, and would hold back their new looks for her. She never paid full price. Having her walk from their store in a new outfit was the best advertising any boutique could hope for. All she had to do was unbutton her top, just one, or maybe two, and teachers, the males and the lesbians, would raise her grades. It seemed like she couldn't turn on the television without seeing her own lovely face, smiling, selling shoes and hats and everything in between.

When she walked in to the Apatite Palace Megachurch, she wasn't surprised that she walked out on the arm of the Rev. Amran Nordlichen, the horribly handsome face of the Pray Like U Mean Business television network. At that moment, it had seemed only natural that her beautiful face would wake every morning with America's favorite, and most holy, face.

There was no doubting it, 18 and 19 were the best years of life for a pretty girl.

Just are surely, there was no doubting that it all went downhill, and went downhill fast from there, and that by 22 it was over. The accident, and the damage to her face, had taken everything from her. She had been poised to become the trophy wife of America's most watched early morning televangelist before being tossed against the glass of her car when rear-ended. After that, well, the pain was too intense to think about after that, at least on most days. Eventually, naturally, she'd been replaced. She had to be replaced. Her Ranny, the Rev. Amran had God's work to do. She dreamed she would be a part of that. It had been a difficult lesson to learn, but it had been a clear message.

The life of a pretty girl ends when the lives of others are just beginning.

She knew this now. Looking back, it was obvious that even before the accident, her life had been slipping away from her. The heads didn't turn as often. Her coffees had started costing the same as they cost everyone else. Newer, fresher, pretty faces, were selling her shoes on television. The camera lingered on stained glass, or even the choir, instead of the fiancée during broadcasts.

But she had to admit that after the problems, she'd been in a freefall. By the time she was 25, she couldn't even inspire a wolf whistle while walking past a construction site, and lord knows she tried.

Chrissy understood that other people lived their whole lives like this. But other people didn't experience life as a pretty, young woman. Other people didn't know the thrill of having a smile so perfect that flashing it made the days of other people.

Nothing on this Earth that could match the pain of losing that attention. By the time she reached 30, she woke each morning suffering and went to bed each night still suffering, yearning for a time when she was "it" but knowing she never would be again.

She'd been desperate, but then it dawned on her that she was focusing only on herself. That's when she'd found Debby. That's when she realized it was too late to spare herself the pain of diminishing, but it was not too late for so many girls who were just like she had been.

She could help them. She could save them from the pain she had to endure. She could save them. She couldn't save them all. But she could save those who reminded her most of herself, who had that twinkle in their eye.

Her girls would never fade. They would never sag or puff or face the heartbreak of scars or wrinkles. They would be, forever, perfect. Their legacies were built on beauty and they would remain beautiful, forever.

They would never wake up to a head turned away from them, a lover who'd lost interest as they dipped into the range of 7s, or something even lower. Instead, in photos and memories, they would always remain "that beautiful girl" and "that perfect piece of ass."

They would forever be lucky enough to have had their last conversations with a stranger begin with "Are you a model?" Luckier still, they'd have been able to have answered that question by saying "Yes."

Chrissy felt a single tear rolling down her cheek as she stood above Carol, who's eyes were now fluttering, just a bit.

Chrissy grasped the statuette by the waste, as she'd learned was best. The breasts formed a wonderful grip. She raised it high above her head. She whispered "Don't worry, they won't see you like this."

She paused to think about the beauty in the tub. Carol was wonderful. Chrissy really liked her. She knew it was bad form to pick favorites. What would the other girls think? She really tried hard to avoid such thinking. Still, there was something special about Carol.

Maybe it was the similar way their mouths turned up, just so, in photos. Maybe it was that they'd both been Garden Sweethearts. It was, Chrissy thought, the first time she'd been back to her old home state for any reason in six years, and the first time she'd ever worked, really worked here.

Maybe that was it, so many connections. She thought about the differences. Carol was perfect and buxom and full hipped. She'd have been chubby within years, so today was a good time to get to her. She was blonde, and her hair was so nicely curled. It was a nest of beautiful, bouncy curls. Playful and sexy and innocent. It was a daring look, a retro look. Chrissy approved.

Chrissy was a brunette and the most her sadly straight hair had ever allowed was a slight, subtle, curl around her face. It had been a perfect frame for her, but it had taken close to an hour each morning. Still, even natural beauties aren't beautiful naturally, she thought.

"Well done, Carol Rose," she said. "You will be remembered as the beauty you are."

She pressed the plastic tarp down around Carol Rose's face, pressing in make sure she's created a good seal. Then she waited. Every couple of minutes she checked the pulse, just to make sure. She continued pressing down on the plastic for a good 10 minutes after the pulse had stopped. When she'd finished, as always, she removed and folded up the tarp, put it away in the bag. Then she aired kissed Carol and fished the phone from her pocket to take a photo. Then she draped Carol's comforter over her. She placed one of Carol's glamor shots on top of her, and slid an identical one into the bag with her statuette.

"We did well here, I think," she told herself as she turned towards the door to leave.

Chapter 9

December 13 10:22 a.m.

"Is it too much to ask of a scholar that they know even the basics about their own subjects," The Professor wondered aloud.

The answer was, of course, "No, it is not too much to ask" but that wasn't what young Emily Bliss was babbling on about.

"I only wrote that to get the scholarship," she said, or at least that's what he thought he made out between her tears. "It was only $500. I don't know any more. I wasn't supposed to know any more! Why are you doing this?"

The anger The Professor felt at that was intense. Technically, it had not been a proper question on his part, just a general musing about the state of American youth.

"Even so," he muttered as he lashed out, nicking her arm and eliciting a sharp scream. "Dum excusare credis, accusas. When we excuse ourselves, we accuse ourselves. I admit I'd heard some rather harsh opinions on the scholarship of Nebraska, but I expected more just outside a university town."

Perhaps, though, the fault lay also with him in this case. He had to admit he had stepped outside his usual course of study to discover this student. The National 4-H Journal had seemed like slumming it even when he'd picked up the copy while at the dentist's office last month. Still, the organization represented the United States Department of Agriculture and in that capacity the scholarship produced such as hers on the "History of Corn" had an obligation to be authoritative.

She, clearly, was not, however. In fact, she knew so little about the history of corn that he had quickly tired of this test, and was now simply rushing it towards an inevitable conclusion. Really, it was a shame. He felt so positive about this outing, especially after discovering that Ms. Bliss would be home alone on this day. She'd taken a sick day, with her parents out of town. He supposed he shouldn't have been surprised to discover that she'd faked her illness, and was using this time to "binge-watch" television shows.

He hadn't even had to figure out a clever way of entry in the home. He'd arrived, rang the bell, and she'd answered. A quick slash at her lower leg had downed her. He wondered if perhaps he hadn't managed to slice the Achilles Tendon. Weak body. And it turned out, a weak mind.

Disturbing that institutions should be passing out scholastic awards to such as this.

In the end, he wasn't convinced she had any particular knowledge about the history of corn. "They called it maize," she'd bleated at one point. "This is the cornhusker state," she'd insisted was an answer at another, though he couldn't even recall the questions at this point. She'd been so unprepared that he could hardly even fake an interest in what she was saying.

"Has the modern world been shaped by corn?" he asked.

He'd been prepared to accept, well by this time, pretty much anything addressing the prehistory of Mesoamerica as an answer. If she'd just touched on the domestication of maize as instrumental to permanent settlements replacing camps tracking the always mobile game in what are now the Mexican states of Puebla and Oaxaca, and how that eventually led to the creation and growth of the Mayan, Aztec and Zapotec civilizations, and, well it went on and on, but young Emily Bliss did not.

Instead, she cried and complained that "I don't know. Leave me alone, please. Please stop hurting me" or some such nonsense. Typical, he thought.

"A classic case of the gladiator waiting until in the arena to come up with a strategy," he said as he contemplated his final questions. "Gladiator in arena consilium capit."

The world of the scholar demands constant vigilance.

But he did wonder if, perhaps, her physical condition didn't play a role in her mental failings.

"Should I start considering physical condition in choosing students," he wondered. "It is a thought worth considering."

This one was, he now realized, pathetic, and pathetic in so many ways. She hadn't correctly answered a single question, or even given him an answer upon which he could muse for a while before rejecting. At the same time, she was asthmatic, at least, and didn't look as if she'd been outside in quite a while.

He thought of the subject. Really, quite creative and certainly quite rich as a topic. Perhaps the History of Corn is a bit too broad for any young mind, but even if her research hadn't answered any of the big questions he was asking, it should have at least prompted her to think about such matters.

Truly a shame, in all regards. His mind wandered through cornfields, connecting civilizations over these past 9,000 years, and considered cultivation as an early and vital example of bio-engineering, and when his mind returned to the present he realized he had already finished the exam, and was just finishing up the pre-exam cleaning up ritual.

"If nothing else," he concluded, "I can thank her for the topic sentence. She may have been a dullard, but the topic was enough to amuse for at least the last 45 minutes."

He wondered, briefly, if he'd actually finished the exam before pronouncing failure. That would, after all, be a fairly serious breach of protocol. But, he acknowledged, he must have heard her final answers at some level before ending them and ending the misery of dealing with this one.

"In any case, the end was inevitable," he decided. "I can hardly be blamed for rushing this result."

Chapter 10

April 27 10:15 p.m.

There were times, like this, when the beauty of the world was almost too much for Coach Carl.

Sitting in his camper van, under a night sky with a blazing bright moon and more stars than city folk ever would imagine, staring at the towering plateaus of Utah's canyon country and with the reassuring hum of his generator and the precious deep freezes it was supporting from the back.

"There is so much beauty in this world," he said to himself. "There is so much wonder and awe and here I sit, as always, alone, knowing I have so much to share but knowing that this path I walk is a lonely one."

Coach Carl was a large, strong man. He had the chest and shoulders of a college linebacker (which he had been), and a co-worker had once told him he had a Dick Tracy jaw.

He was handsome, in the way that a boxer who'd had a few too many fights against folks who punched just a bit too hard could be handsome. His was a lived-in body. His face was one that had seen more of this world than most men could dream of seeing in a lifetime. Co-workers had told him this. His mom had told him this. He took it all as a compliment.

Why take the words in any other way, he thought. People are basically good, they want to be good.

And yet, here he was, only 44 years old.

There was no doubt about that. He took that as a compliment. He was also a man who had experienced moments of great beauty in his life.

Many of them. There was the 1999 Kansas state championship 4x400 relay race. His girls had not been the fastest in that race, but they'd ran an almost perfect relay. Each girl beat their previous best time, and the handoffs were more like liftoffs. A perfect light rain had been falling on the University of Kansas track, though the sun was in a patch of blue sky.

The rain, it made the air look as if it was dropping diamonds. The bigger schools, the faster kids, looked sloppy. That was a disappointment. Coach Carl always wanted everyone at their very best. He never wanted to win by default. He wanted to win because his people were perfect. On that day, his girls almost were. Though, on that day, he hadn't won at all. In the end, a faster girl, a girl who had been granted by nature with a pace his girls simply could not match, had stormed in front of his team on the final stretch. By the end of that straightaway, she was leading by three strides.

That was, he knew, his fate. To come so close, to see his coaching imbue an almost transcendent beauty to his athletes, yet to fail. Still, on that day, so very beautiful. So close to perfect that they'd inspired him every day since, inspired his project.

Then there was the buzzer beater from distance, a solid 23 feet, by his first donor. His team had been up by two, with 24 seconds left in the match, and had been inbounding the ball. The Class AAA state championship on the line, but seemingly in the bag. The only time Coach Carl's boys ever got to a state final in basketball. This was a legacy game, and until the last seconds, his boys were bringing it to him. Twenty three seconds remained when the inbounds landed in the hands of his captain. He spun and made the exact right pass and moved to receive the return, again perfect and switched the ball from the right to the left side of the court. It was a perfect play, carving open the St. Matthew's team. It was evidence that his boys were better prepared and better honed. St. Matthew's players were spinning in circles trying to follow them. Then on the sixth rapid pass, with only five seconds left, Danny Seibel stepped into the lane, nabbed the pass and was racing off downcourt.

His team had been a symphony. Young Mr. Seibel was a solo act. His strides quick and confident. He was completely aware of the game clock and court. He pulled up just in front of the three-point line. His body was perfect, his form was perfect. The ball left his hand and halfway through its arc the buzzer went. But there was never any doubt in Coach's mind where the ball would end up. By the time it had nestled into the net, igniting wild celebrations from the other side, Coach knew that once again, nature had bested his nurture. Seibel was perfect. He was graceful under pressure. His thinking had been stunningly quick and his execution had been perfectly assured.

Coach had to admit, it was another moment of beauty, though one again mixed with pain.

At that moment, Coach was overwhelmed by the need to possess that sort of athlete. He's perfect, Coach thought.

But in the hours that followed, he realized young Seibel fell short of perfection in several areas. His perfection had been in analyzing and remaining calm. He had a better head for the game than any player Coach had ever coached, or could remember. But his legs didn't have the spring of explosive quickness of others. His arms and chest were far from perfectly strong.

"But that head, it's amazing," he thought.

Six months later, Coach was on a hunting trip 200 miles from home, hiding in a thicket waiting on a tom turkey, when a loud snore off to his right had scared away the bird. Angered, he'd looked for the source and found it was none other than Seibel, clearly drunk, armed with a shotgun and in full camo. He should be wearing orange, Coach thought. This is dangerous. He shook him awake.

"Come on, young man, you should get up and join your party and go home."

"Jeez. Is it morning? We were out all night. They must have left me."

"You're alone out here?"

"Looks like it, doesn't it old man?"

"But you're the basketball captain…"

"What? That shit is over, too long ago to matter. Now I just want to sleep some more."

Seibel, clutching his shotgun like a child would clutch a teddy bear, rolled back over. The shotgun had been wedged against his neck when it went off. Seibel was clearly dead, almost decapitated.

Coach remembered the sadness of that moment. It started in his heart, but spread throughout his body. Here was a young athlete, with a great head for sport, and he'd been throwing away all that potential.

But in the dawn on that morning, as he looked at that perfect head for sport literally now at his feet, he realized that all athletes would eventually disappoint. They would meet somebody better, with more natural gifts. Or they would age, or be injured.

But this sort of beauty, this sort of perfection? That would last. Coach used the sack he'd hoped to fill with a turkey to pick up the head that had been delivered to him. He fit that into his backpack. He cleared away any sign that he'd been in the thicket, which was easy enough.

Ten months later, he got a call from the Topeka Capitol Journal. A sportswriter he'd known for years wanted to know if he'd heard the news, that Danny Seibel had died in a hunting accident. He wanted to know if Coach would like to offer a quote for an article he was writing on the tragic and untimely death.

"He was a gift," Coach said, without pause. "The way he saw basketball, he was an artist. He had that rarest of traits, a perfect head for the game."

The writer had thanked Coach for his time, but changed the wording from "head" to "understanding." Saying head would have been unkind to the family, when it appeared critters had carried the head away from the body. "But how was Coach to know that."

After that phone call, Coach had gone down into his basement and opened his deep freeze. Young Seibel's head still looked about like it had on the day it had been presented to him, he thought. But a head, alone in the deep freeze? That was incomplete. That was lonely.

That had been another moment of surpassing beauty for Coach. Having pushed aside bags of frozen corn and pot-stickers, he looked down at Danny, knew what the fates wanted from him. Even the best of those he'd seen, in person or on television, would fade eventually.

"Unless, I preserve them, at their peak," he thought.

That was the moment he realized his mission. He'd always known he was on Earth to build better young bodies, to put together athletes, to always aspire towards perfection. He'd always admired, to the point of obsession, those with the highest levels of natural gifts in sport. Still, each and every one of those he'd admired had a weakness.

"I will build athletes without weakness," he thought. "A girl and a boy. I will build the perfect tribute to greatness."

That was how it had started, with the gift of Danny Seibel in a field in Kansas. In the years since, Coach had expanded his reach, and his search, to complete his tributes. Eventually, he realized he couldn't do it all from his house. There were too many risks of transporting a leg or arm or torso 1,000 miles in the trunk of his car. It wasn't respectful, first off.

So he'd bought this camper van and modified it. The bed rested on his two large deep freezes. They sucked up a lot of energy, so he'd had to build a decent generator into the van to handle that. He was quite proud of that setup, fed by the solar panels on the van roof, with a nicely vented and super quiet gas backup that kicked on when the sun set.

The freezers rested below his bed. Beyond that, the van had a small stove and a toilet/shower stall. He was proud of the van, though the real joy in life rested in the coolers.

His boys´ cooler, as of two hours ago, was finished. He'd needed a left leg and he'd seen the clips of his spectacular triple jumper in Beaver, Utah. He'd come and watched him in person. Amazing lift. Really, he could have used more than the left leg. But he'd made the rules, no more than one piece per athlete. Make sure you know the athletes well enough to ensure they're worthy of their spot in the tribute. There was no point in adding a right-handed discus thrower to the collection if you already had a right-handed quarterback's arm.

There was no need to be wasteful. It just required careful planning. He'd long since accepted that the tribute might not represent the absolute best the United States had to offer, but it would certainly represent nothing but the elite athletes he so admired.

His perfect boy was now finished. Danny's head, with the eyes of a golfer. One hand from a leftie baseball pitcher, a right hand from a three point specialist in basketball. A quarterback's left arm, a shot putter´s right. The torso of a 148 pound wrestler. The right leg of place-kicker and the left of a hurdler.

He'd debated whether feet played into it was well, but decided that while with hands they changed everything about the way a ball rotated or a curveball broke, feet relied more on the entire dynamic of the leg. Nine donors, in all.

All nine were all state, though from eight different states.

He was quite proud of his boy. He would match him up against any collection, anywhere, against any athlete. In his fantasies, science would advance to the point where he could animate his tribute. But he knew that was unlikely to ever happen. As it was, he was happy with what he considered a job well done. It was art, in its purest form.

"There was no skimping in his project," he thought, and the thought made him beam. He considered opening a beer to celebrate. That would be breaking protocol, however, and he was nothing if not disciplined. Despite the excitement at the thought of completing the project, he'd always limited himself to no more than two pieces per school year, and he always waited until the end of a year because spring sports mattered. He'd decided in the beginning to work boy-girl, boy-girl, and he'd maintained that.

No boy and girl came from the same school, or even state.

In any case, it was not truly time yet to celebrate. The boy was complete. The girl still needed a left leg. He would have to get his van back home in time to coach practice in two days. And he had work to do on the project.

He thought about the donors in the girls' collection in the back. The head had been a wonderful point guard. The eyes had been an archer. The torso an Olympic alternate gymnast. The right leg had been a sprinter. The right hand had been a softball player, again a pitcher. The right arm had been a volleyball player, quite a spike. The left hand had been a tennis phenom. The left arm was rather remarkable, a champion arm wrestler, only 18. His work was almost complete.

"The left leg should be a soccer player," he thought. "I've got some research to do."

He turned around and addressed the girl's tribute freezer.

"Don't worry, we will find your missing piece soon," he said. Then he turned to address his boy. "And don't you worry, either. You'll have company soon enough."

Chapter 11

Nov. 20 5:34 p.m.

Nev pulled her backpack and dress carrier from the back of her Mom's car and took off walking towards the Miss Teen Colorado finals in Snack Hall on the campus of The Women's College of Colorado.

This was not Nev's ideal way to spend a Saturday evening. It was not even close to ideal. But her Mom had been concerned that with study and soccer, she didn't take any time out to be a girl. Nev thought this was a weird sentiment, but nine months earlier, her mom came to her with the sign-up material. Nev had figured there were worse fates.

There were 20 regions in the Colorado contest. Nev was in region 17. Region 17 had never won the state contest.

The notion that Nev would win even on the Region 17 level was absurd. Nev had heard girls at school talk about these things, and they required a skill set Nev didn't have, and wasn't willing to work to acquire.

But in any case, her Mom didn't expect her to win. She wanted Nev to put on makeup for once. She wanted Nev to wear a pretty dress.

"For one weekend, just focus on being a girl," her mom asked when she came with the sign-up stuff.

So when the letter came telling Nev she's actually won Region 17 and qualified for the state contest, it was a bit of surprise.

First, it had been a surprise because she thought there would have been an actual contest. When her mom called the Region 17 organizers they told her "Not this year. No need this year."

Her mom was thrilled, convinced that their paperwork had been exceptional.

Nev wondered to her mom if she'd been "the only girl who entered."

"Maybe this is why Region 17 has never won," Nev thought. "Maybe no one ever enters."
Nev wasn't really sure how these things worked, after all.

But today, as she neared Snack Hall, which would host the statewide contest, she realized both she and her mom had focused on the wrong part of the question about whether other girls had entered the contest.

Thousands of protesters surrounded the building. Angry young woman carried signs saying "End Sexism Now." Topless middle-aged women chanted "Brains not Boobs." Hundreds of what looked to be college guys had shown up in drag, carrying signs that "This is what Pageantry Looks Like" Most stunning of all were the 16 of those guys in ball gowns, wearing sashes. The sashes were all similar to one Nev had saying Region 17, except theirs proclaimed "Region 1" or "Region 20" or all except four regions in between. Nev blushed a little when she realized two of the guys had the exact gown she'd picked out for the contest.

She also noted the television news cameras had gathered on the far side of the building, and could see reporters talking into microphones under bright lights. She also noticed three other girls, who like her, had arrived with a suitcase and a dress bag. The girls were standing in a huddle on the outskirts of the protest. Nev thought they looked very much like the girls she thought would win contests like this. They saw her bag and dress bag and motioned for her to join them.

"You look like you're going inside," one said as she arrived. "Do you work with Miss Teen? Can you help us get in?"

"Uhm, no, I don't work for them, but I am going in."

"How?"

"Well, I'm going to walk."

"But FWB is in the way. They'll stop you."

"FWB?"

"Fully Woke, Brah."

"Which is?"

"The Colorado fraternity what swore to shut down the pageant this year. All those guys in dresses. They're saying it's sexist and wrong and has to stop. I, mean, I spent a year getting ready for this. I wish they could have stopped it next year."

Nev had no idea what they were talking about, and said so.

"Didn't you see the pageant warnings? Don't you read the pageant news?"

Nev had to admit that she had skipped those items. What she learned was the Beta Rho Omicron fraternity at the University of Colorado had, at first as a joke, decided to shut down the Miss Teen Beauty pageant as sexist.

The immediate result was that on campus, the fraternity members became instant heroes to women's rights groups, and overnight their fraternity parties improved exponentially.

Once they started making a serious effort to shut down the pageant they found that they had members and allies who could make quite a difference. Their computer science majors were able to disable websites around the state, all 20 regions were officially put offline. Their law school alumni were able to successfully challenge the "female" only status of the contest and force the recognition of males as entrants.

Their journalism and criminal law majors had managed to track down almost every entrant in the state, and convince them to give the pageant a pass this year.

In the end, they'd only missed four girls, and those four were given regional titles without publicity and without a public ceremony in the hopes that they could remain anonymous until the official pageant. The state organizers had paid up front for the hall and the flowers and, well, everything, and they didn't want to cancel and be out what amounted to $43,257.

So, at the very least, they had hoped to sneak four girls onto the stage.

But they hadn't anticipated the protest expand beyond the fraternity crowd, or to be so large and committed. They also hadn't expected their four girls to be so completely overwhelmed.

As Nev stood in the small group looking at the intensity of the protest build, one of the contestants (Region 8) looked up and said, "Fuck this. Maybe they're right. Maybe they're stupid, but I am not walking through that mess. Nothing is worth that."

As she walked away, a second of the girls started crying, then starting crying a lot harder. Nev put an arm around her shoulders.
"It's okay, it's going to be fine. She made her choice, you make your own. And all these protestors, they're just venting. They're not really dangerous."

Region 4 didn't seem at all sure about that. She shook Nev's arm off her shoulders and shouted, "No, she was right. This is stupid. This wasn't my dream. My dream is ruined."

She then turned to the protesting crowd, shouted "I hope you're happy" and stormed off in the direction of Region 8.

"Huh, just us. Region 17 and Region … which one are you from?"

"Region 19," the girl answered, but she was sniffling.

Nev didn't know that the protesters were wrong in their general view on pageants. This wasn't her dream, after all. But she didn't think it was fair of them to take out their anger on this girl. Region 19 was not to blame for sexism in the world, after all.

"Okay, then, now, we're going in."

Nev grabbed the bag from Region 19 and put her free arm around her, then started walking towards the entrance. She was thinking it might be better to pack it in, as well, but she'd promised her mom and a promise was a promise.

"Should we be doing this?" the girl asked.

"Yeah, if we don't, we are going to be late."

"It's good to be late if the alternative is getting murdered."

"We aren't going to be murdered. We aren't victims here, we're just two bad-ass girls walking through an angry crowd. It's going to be fine. We will be fine. Nothing will happen to us."

Looking back on it, Nev realized that was a bit of an overstatement. Quite a bit happened. They had lots of cardboard signs thrust into their faces, and Region 19 even took a small cut on the cheek from one. Twice, people ripped the garment bags from Nev's hand, and twice she had to look really fiercely into people's eyes in order to convince them to return the bags.

Someone even unzipped Nev's backpack and removed her talent prop, but as it was a soccer ball the thief figured it was unlikely to have anything to do with the contest and threw it at her as they were squeezing between the security guards and climbing the wide stone step leading to the Snack Hall entrance.

In the end, her mom couldn't make it into the building, which sucked. Not many people could.

In fact, when Regions 17 and 19 came through the door, the three judges who had managed to get inside were just discussing how to cancel the pageant without letting the protesters know that they'd won. They were also discussing whether they could somehow proclaim a victory for Miss Teen if they crowned one of the guys.

Still, two of the judges had squealed with laughter when they saw the girls walk into the backstage area. The third had wiped tears from her eyes.

The audience consisted of the official photographers and videographer and eight others who Nev was pretty sure just happened to be working in the building and had come down to check out the chaos. About two thirds of the way through the very abbreviated contest (they were told to expect to last three hours, but were done in 28 minutes), a small group of protesters burst into the auditorium but because there wasn't much going on allowed themselves to be escorted right back out the door.

Nev was surprised at the protest, and really surprised that most of the contestants were guys in dresses. But she admitted to herself there was no surprise when the guys who had worked so hard to disrupt the pageant showed no interest at all in anything beyond walking on to the stage and chanting for a couple minutes.

After that, they walked off the stage and out to a cheering crowd where they declared victory and prepared for a night of pretty intense partying.

So it wasn't much of a contest. Still, a lot of photos were taken, and a professionally done video produced. They didn't show the lack of a crowd, so when her mom finally got to see the contest, she was pleased and convinced her daughter had finally had a single day of "just being a girl."

The press release on the event didn't mention the problems they'd encountered, just noted the winner and the runner up, and was quite vague about any other details. The protest was top of the hour news on television, and front-page news for the newspaper websites. But the much shorter winners list was still mentioned and the crowning photo popped up on quite a few news sites.

Despite the fact that there were only two girls on stage, and one was bleeding and crying through the whole ceremony, her mom beamed when she found out Nev had been crowned the winner. Her mom thought Nev "looked just lovely" in her red gown and even acknowledged that her "keepy-uppy" juggling with the soccer ball while wearing that gown was a very impressive talent display.

Nev had to admit, the whole day had been pretty funny, at least looking back on it. She figured she could scold herself over the fact that she'd somehow managed to miss a ton of news that would have warned her to stay away from the event. Almost no one else had shown up even for the regionals, after all.

But, as her mom suggested, the title might help with some college applications to show that she was well rounded, and at the very least, she drove home that night with a good story to tell.

Chapter 12

May 18th 1:18 p.m.

Nev was more than a little scared. The Piggly Wiggly had been a good call. The Fast 'n' Quick was okay for a single snack, but the costs added up when you were buying by the shopping cart full. And the variety was better at the Pig.

That wasn't the problem. She'd come in under budget. Not that she really had a budget. Her Mom and Dad had left a wad of cash to handle all expenses, and she wasn't sure she could figure out a way to spend it all, at least not in Chances.

It wasn't the money. It was the volume that was scaring her.

The ranch chips had seemed like a good idea at the time, as had the jalapeno chips, and the salt and vinegar, and the soft cookies. And the Chunky Monkey.

Taken separately, she still believed they were solid decisions. This was, after all, her reward. She had just completed a senior year of high school during which she hadn't taken 10 minutes for herself. She studied. In fact, she'd gone a bit overboard on the studying. The year was a bit of a jumble in her mind right now, but she was pretty sure it was the studying that had set the pace for her frantic year.

It had started simply enough. A history assignment to do a paper highlighting a little-known facet of a well-known historical figure that shaped that figure's worldview. Her senior year was new at that point, so she'd decided to go all in on the project.

She'd ended up at the Eastern Colorado University library, after the soccer coach had asked her to come by and take a look at the school. She was aimlessly strolling the stacks looking for names she recognized when she came across an eight-volume psychological profile of Abraham Lincoln. That, she'd decided, was a good a place to start as anywhere.

Before she was a quarter of the way through, she had her idea. Lincoln, as a little kid, was visiting a neighbor's farm in Little Pigeon Creek when one of their sows gave birth to a litter. Lincoln watched, fascinated. After the birth, the farmer separated one little pig, the smallest of the bunch, from the others.

"Why are you doing that?" the future president asked.

"He's the runt of the litter," the farmer answered. "He'll die anyway, so it's best to make it quick."

Lincoln had been horrified. None of God's creatures should simply be abandoned, he'd thought. He asked instead if he could have the runt to raise as his own. The farmer agreed, and Abe, having no other way of transporting the piglet, had wrapped it in the front of his long shirt and run home with it to show his parents.

Nancy and Thomas Lincoln had treated this flight of fancy by their son as all parents in all times treat the thrill of a found pet by their children. They told him the pig was a big responsibility, and that feeding and caring for it would fall entirely upon him.

For the first month of the pig's life, Abe would wrap it back into his longshirt and return, twice a day, to the neighbor's farm to feed the pig. Then he would forage for food for it on his own, berries to table scraps. The pig grew, and by the next summer was three times the weight of Abe. For much of that next summer, neighbors found great joy in watching young Abe ride his pig around the community. The two were inseparable. He even earned the nickname "Pigboy."

Nev had read that and realized, if the story ended there, it was an example of how Lincoln learned to believe in the value of every individual. She thought it was possible to talk about his eventual opposition to slavery.

But the story didn't end there. Later that summer, Thomas had told Abe he'd done a fine job with the pig, but it was now time to butcher and eat it. Abe cried and begged his father not to follow through. The following morning, before his father made it outside to the barn to slaughter the pig, Abe took it and raced into the woods. They hid all day, and at night Abe returned with a plan to do the same the next morning.

But the next morning, Thomas put a nose ring to the pig, and staked it to the ground. Little Abe hadn't been strong enough to pull out the stake. When he saw his father come out, and heard him at the grinder sharpening his knife, Abe had fled alone. Throughout his life, he would maintain that the sound of his pig's final cry haunted him.

"From that moment on, I ate neither ham nor bacon, chop nor loin," Lincoln had once said.

Nev found the story horrifying, and heartbreaking, and wrote a paper that offered this as a foundational base for the man who became a great president.

The paper had been more than a bit of a success. Beyond a wildly enthusiastic A, her history teacher insisted she enter it in a national contest, and it had won that, as well. She'd won a Colorado Scholar contest, which came with a very cool translucent trophy that looked like a mountain. Then she'd been awarded a President's Council on Academic Excellence medal, which came with a star shaped medal on a red, white and blue ribbon. She'd even gone to Denver and Washington D.C. to pick up the awards. It was all accidental, really, but it had been a thrill.

Somehow it had led to the beauty pageant. She wasn't really sure how. She blamed her mom. Her mom had been convinced that Nev was too wrapped up in studies and soccer, and that she needed to just enjoy being a teenage girl for a change. So she'd signed Nev up for the Junior Miss Colorado pageant. Nev knew her Mom meant well, so she took part in the local version. She even liked that she could juggle a soccer ball with her feet for the talent portion. She won, so she agreed to go on to the statewide version of the contest.

She won the statewide contest, as well. It came with money for college, $5,000 a year in scholarship, so it wasn't a total waste. It was a long way from a total waste, actually. But she was still a bit embarrassed at taking part. At school, she didn't really have friends, but she did have teammates. She didn't tell a soul, but The Denver Post ran an article on their Sunday entertainment page. No kid she knew, of course, saw that, but their parents all did. And her teachers all did. And it was online, and on Facebook and, well, she got a lot of money for college out of the deal, and she made her Mom really happy so it was worthwhile.

Her biggest time suck, however, was soccer. She knew that. She also knew it was her first and primary love. She loved the thunk of the ball on her left foot when she sent in a long cross. She loved the smell of the grass as she slid through an opponent and came up with the ball and ready to run. She loved the freedom of sprinting down a sideline away from the ball, of seeing backs turned away from her, eyes on the ball and ignoring the defender blasting full speed down the empty sideline, and towards the box. She loved it when her team spotted her and the ball came soaring, getting lost for a second in the lights, or the sun, before she'd find it again and adjust her run to meet it full force, with her head, with a foot, sometimes with a knee and once with her butt, and the thunk, whoosh of the ball snapping into the net. Of course, she didn't score much. She was a defender, a left back, who loved bombing down the field into the attack.

She loved defending. She loved being the best player on the field and the hardest player on the field and the fastest. Her room had a wall devoted to trophies and photos. It was a collection she started building at 7, and that now had a freaking All-America centerpiece that had been announced a week ago, and two All-Colorado plaques. More importantly, her fall club team had qualified for the Dallas Cup, and gotten wasted but still, they played. And her high school team had won regionals, and lost a state championship on penalty kicks (so, technically, she believed, they tied. PKs were crap, even if she'd made hers).

She missed soccer when she wasn't playing. She didn't really have friends outside of her teams. Her closest friends were from regional team camps, and lived hundreds of miles away.

But right now, she was tuning out from even soccer. She went after her senior year, and crushed it, and now she was, well, really tired.

She'd been looking forward to this time alone all year, as well. It was as much a part of her plan on how to get after her last year of high school as the books or the makeup or the practice. From as far back as she could remember, Mom and Dad had been complaining about how hard their lives were. She didn't doubt it. They sure seemed busy all the time.

Brody was a surprise, a really early surprise. They'd never said as much, but doing the math and having seen their wedding photos, it was pretty clear Brody had been crazy early, and her Mom and Dad had married at 18. Eighteen? She couldn't imagine a scenario which would see her getting married now, rather than getting ready to get snuggled down in the couch with an insane amount of junk food.

Brody, the story went, arrived before Mom and Dad were quite ready, and when they were still poor. "Fish-sticks, four nights a week, and the cheap ones, in the big box," Mom had explained, telling her about the time before Nev arrived. "That's how poor we were. You never had to live that, we were doing well by the time you got here. It was tough."

Which was true. Nev's life was busy, and intense and filled with pressure, but she also knew it was easy. She never had to eat cheap breaded fish-sticks, except at school where she kind of liked them. That was really about as far as the "we were so poor" stories ever got, but Nev imagined there were parts left unsaid. She'd seen the movies. Maybe Mom was a stripper, she thought, then giggled.

Though there was one constant piece of that story beyond fish-sticks. They were so poor that they couldn't afford a honeymoon. Their honeymoon had been two nights at the Highway Motel 35 miles down the road in Humboldt. Their first meal as a married couple had been the all you can eat buffet at La Hacienda.

Her Mom told her this, many times, and always in the soft, sad voice usually reserved for tragic news, like when Grandma died. It was a bit odd, though, because even the day before they finally left on their real honeymoon, so two days ago, they'd taken her out for dinner at La Hacienda, as a treat.

The real point of this memory, though, was that Nev had always known that as soon as she'd graduated from high school, as soon as she was old enough that leaving her alone for a couple weeks wouldn't be illegal, they were gonna take off.

"Long gone, like a turkey in the corn," her Dad always said. It was a weird thing to say. He would pronounce "corn" more like "con." Still, he always seemed impressed with himself when he said it, so she'd smile. Her parents were goofy, but she loved them. She didn't mind being on her own, though.

She looked at her setup. Nice big flat screen, connected to a glowing neon retro looking sound system. Two empty overstuffed chairs. A wide couch with a million big pillows. A fuzzy red blanket. And a coffee table that was pretty much a garbage dump, though with unopened chips.

Nev could take care of herself. She realized the mountain of different chips might not make that case very well. But she had earned this. She wondered why she was alone.

She'd seen the teen movies when someone's parents went on vacation, it was party time. She'd mentioned that to her Dad, and he'd laughed. Then she'd threatened that with her Mom, and she'd laughed. She had to admit that when she'd mentioned before graduation that her parents were leaving her alone for two weeks, the Hollywood stock character who was supposed to pop up yelling "Partay" and making confusing hand signs had been absent.

No one had asked to come over or suggested a party. No one had questioned her parents' judgement at leaving her alone. Instead, people had agreed "Oh, you'll be fine."

It was a bit disappointing, she thought. "I suppose I am a good girl. Can't complain about that too much."

Everyone assumed she would fine. She may have just completed a year of crushing books, babes and balls, but it hadn't really implied anything dangerous about her.

"I suppose they're right," she concluded. She looked at her pile of food and decided that she was going to have to add a pizza to the collection at some point.

She turned on the television and decided on either a Breaking Bad or Criminal Minds marathon. She grabbed the jalapeno chips and ripped open the bag.

Could she have been using this time better? Others might think so. She could have been at the gym, building strength, or working on her cross and fitness. She could get after the summer reading list for college. But her fitness was pretty solid, and she had months to do the reading.

She knew there was nothing wrong with a night all to herself, in which to pamper herself in ways she would not have for the past school year.

She's earned this time to herself. "The biggest problem I'll be facing tonight is gonna be indigestion," she thought. "I can deal with indigestion."

Chapter 13

May 5, 7:01 p.m.

The Professor closed the shades in his study and went to the closet to lug out his trusty overhead projector. It was time to choose his next destination, and the Professor thought that he might just like this stage most of all. The Choice. The possibilities were endless. At this point, The Choice was an empty page, waiting for his quill to forever change it.

He paused to look around. His study was a shaped like an ice-cream cone, though one in which the tip of the cone had broken off. The drippings would have been caught in the huge closet. As with everything the Professor had brought with him from his days of glory, it was exactly the stereotype of what would be expected of someone dedicated only to the pursuit of knowledge, but who just happened to have a lot of money to toss around.

The semi-circle of windows made up the cone. They were the result of the turret in the front of his three-story brownstone near the Boston Common. Back when he'd been making millions from his thesis cum novel cum movie, he bought a full floor of a refined though slightly, if chicly, shabby building. He found the 15-foot-high molded ceilings allowed his thoughts to soar without hindrance. The shine in the oak floors, baseboards and doors kept him rooted. The deep Persian rugs and polished brass and crystal light fixtures and door handles were calming.

Taken together, these seven rooms, cluttered with stacks of books and bookshelves that held precious mementos and honors from a previous life served as a reminder that once he had been to the top of the mountain. He had sipped Louis XIII cognac here with university luminaries and stars from across the academic world. He had poured a wonderful, tannic '61 Bordeaux from the Medoc for Monsieur Pierre de la Pompeux, the brilliant French director who had first turned his work into a substantial film. And he had mixed a very dry martini for Mister Juan Jugar-Montaña, then the darling of Hollywood, as he turned that work into a summer blockbuster film, that left the Professor never again in need of money.

Carrying the projector by its neck he hoisted it onto his polished Cherrywood desk, and pointed it at his prized version of "Bonaparte visiting the plague victims of Jaffa." The original, of course, remained in the Louvre. This was an actual study prepared by Antoine-Jean Gros before he put together the full 15 feet by 21 feet original. The study version, quite a bit smaller but at five feet high and seven wide still dominating the only open wall in his study, was remarkable in its likeness to the original. The professor often thought that if the artist had only had an overhead projector, such as the one he was now carrying, he could simply have copied the smaller image onto the larger one, and saved himself quite a bit of hassle.

As it was, the Professor was quite proud of this work. He had paid an Albanian dealer in off-book antiquities $75,000 for it a decade earlier. His dealer had later been arrested. He'd been arrested by Interpol, actually. The Professor found this quite thrilling. International intrigue implied the Professor led an exciting, mysterious life. The arrest came as part of an international crackdown on those dealing in stolen and forged art. His dealer had told him Gros had only made three studies, and this was the best of them. His Gros study, which surely had a dubious provenance, was off book enough not to be included in the Interpol case. The professor found this to be good news. His good fortune was now even more rare and more impossible for anyone else to get their hands on. As it brought him joy every time he entered this room, it had been worth every penny.

It was quite natural, the Professor thought, that he had therefore incorporated the work into "The Choice." The Choice was equal parts art and science, he thought. The methodology behind it had been quite complicated to arrive at, and now filled most of a Moleskin ledger. He liked that he had decided against total precision in all facets of the process.

He set the projector in roughly, but not exactly, the same spot each time. He leaned over the desk and unlocked a large drawer that appeared to be empty. He tapped the top of the drawer, and what had looked to be a rubber gasket to protect the wood popped up to reveal a small gap inside the wood facing. That gap held a single manila file folder. The folder held a single item, a map of the United States on a slide. The map was an outline, in the fashion of U.S. maps with the 48 contiguous states, roughly to scale, above cutouts of Alaska and Hawaii, which were not at all to scale.

The map was in green, with mountains noted in a slightly darker green, and state borders in a very light green. Aside from the geographic markings, there were 7 red dots. The professor turned on the projector, laying the image of the country over the painting. He picked up a red marker. Using the projected image to guide him more accurately, he added an 8th dot, right about where Silver Spring, Maryland, would be.

He smiled. Out with the old, in with the new. He flipped open the binder, skimming pages until he found a 9 he had circled twice. The cryptic note beside this "why does he ignore the general? Is he rushing to a loved one, and is his cap's tassel a statement of stature beyond his vest?"

The word "tassel" was underlined. Looking back at the painting, he found the man ignoring Napoleon, brushing by the group without a look. He scanned up the body to the cap, and the tassel. Then, as he now knew was necessary, he blinked, to refocus his eyes. He would have to see both map and the tassel, together, instead of just the tassel.

He flipped to the back page of his ledger and on a line noting 9 he wrote down Nixon County, near Denver, Colorado.

"Interesting," he thought. "I remember coming across someone in Colorado."

Having found his location, he now had to find his scholar. Usually, this was the more difficult part of The Choice, and in the past had taken as long as three days of pouring through research papers in library stacks and academic journals, as well as popular media reports on academic excellence. But in this case, he remembered he had come across a name during the search that led him to the late Mr. Nichols.

"Dare I?" he asked as he rifled through his magazine stacks searching for a list of Presidential Scholars. He had not before gone back to the same well, not once. He hadn't really had that chance. The map determined the where, and it had never worked out this way before. This seemed to be fate, and he was not one to ignore fate.

He turned pages in the magazine, scanning for Mr. Nichols name. He found him on page 56. Then he turned the pages back towards the front of the magazine, this time running a finger down the page and looking for the word "Colorado."

On page 49, he found her. A history scholar, he sniffed. Two in a row, both dealing with Lincoln? This was intriguing. She had won the girls prize that was the matched set to Mr. Nichols boy's award. It was a bit too close for The Professor's tastes, but did the map actually bring her to him? She had dealt with an obscure psychological profile of the man, however, and he admired that sort of academic chutzpah. Could it be this simple, he wondered. He looked at her home school,

Chances High School. He went to a book pile and plucked out a detailed atlas. In the index, he found this Chances, and into the book for the actual map.

He found Chances on the map, and within seconds had seen it was indeed in Thomas County. The idea of two scholars from the same magazine gave him pause. But clearly the universe was guiding him.

The final phase of The Choice was now upon him. It was always a surprise. He opened another drawer in his desk and grabbed his yearly planner. He flipped through pages until he was pinching shut the days of this year already passed.

He took his favorite Montblanc from a Yardton coffee mug on the desk and closed his eyes. As he began flipping through the pages of the year yet to come, he let the pen fall. May 18th. Not much time, but enough. As she was his ninth scholar, he made a notation at 9 p.m. Perfect, he thought. It's scheduled.

He looked at the photo accompanying the article announcing her victory and smiled.

"Hello Nev Sparrow of Chances, Colorado," he said in an almost loving voice. "I can't wait to meet you."

Chapter 14

May 2, 7:56 a.m.

The space between Chrissy Kristen's pink faux fur covered comforter and pillows to her bedazzled computer monitor and desk was fit for a princess. At least, that had been the plan when she was setting it up.

The rest of her two-room bungalow was simply depressing and Chrissy didn't like to think about things such as the leaking drain in the kitchen, or the loose tiles covering the back of her shower.

Chrissy found it appalling that she could be asked to think about such things. Her small house was sparkly clean. She prided herself on that. But repairs? Life just wasn't fair. That had never been her destiny.

She should have had a rich husband paying for repairmen at their mansion by this point in her life.

She had that, before the accident. She paused to correct herself, almost. She almost had that. It was painful, even to remember. On the other hand, it was impossible to forget.

She had been foolish, she supposed. She thought he'd still love her after her deformities became clear as doctors unwrapped the bandages. Ranny, or rather the Rev. Amran Nordlichen to her these days, had said it wouldn't matter. That he didn't love her for what was visible to the world, for what he alone could see in her.

Such crap. She could see the look of complete disappointment in his eyes when the doctor unveiled New Chrissy. Just like with New Coke, she had become hard to love. He'd never really looked her in the eyes again after that moment.

She should have seen the signs that he was leaving. She should have, but she was busy feeling sorry for herself. The signs had been there. Before the accident, she had been moving closer and closer to Ranny during services and had started to appear on the fringes of the Whole Glory in the Morning Show on P.L.U.M.B. She'd never been by his side. She was a fiancée, not a member of the inner circle.

The Reverends Tommy and Laurie Cobbleer would stand with him at their tri-lectern in the Amarite Church altar, with the stunning blues and reds of the stained glass wall behind them on fire from the first lights of dawn. They would hold hands and beseech God to provide his grace, and give them the strength and resources to do his work.

No, she never got that far front and center in Ranny's world. She never expected that. These were three of the most famous faces of God in the United States. Ranny was the most-high, of course, but Laurie's deeply rouged cheeks, purple lips and bright blue eye-shadowed face was almost as famous. Tommy, who's own makeup was a regal orange, was known around the world for his fierce condemnation of sodomites.

Chrissy knew the signs had been there. One day she'd be asked to take a suit to the cleaners to remove the purple lipstick, blue eyeshadow and rouge that had smeared over the fly in the pants when Laurie during a quick change had needed something to blot her tears for the "starving little brown babies" somebody needed to help. The next day, Chrissy would be headed back to the cleaners because almost the same thing had happened to a different suit pant when Tommy during another quick change had lost control of his emotions while lamenting the sodomite control of Congress.

Eventually, Tommy and Laurie had moved into Ranny's mansion with him, and her place in the house that was supposed to be their home had been reduced and reduced and reduced until, eventually, it vanished.

"Chrissy, you don't really work in this setting," Ranny had explained finally.

"Is it because of my scars," she asked, almost apologetically. "I know I'm hideous now."

Ranny had paused for a few minutes before he responded. Chrissy knew he'd been trying to figure out some way of saying what he had to say to her without hurting her too badly.

"Your face threatens the church," he'd finally said. "People see your deformity, and know the beauty you used to possess, and question God. We can't have that. When people stop helping the church, we can no longer help the starving little brown babies. When people turn off their televisions, the sodomites take full control of Congress. We can't have that. You don't want that."

Through her sobs, Chrissy had asked whether she couldn't possibly cover up her horrible mouth with makeup, but Ranny had a point when he noted that Tommy and Laurie were already known for their makeup, and there really wasn't another place in the inner circle for anything new, or a copy job.

When Chrissy had suggested she could exist in the dark shadows cast by the glow his life, Ranny had explained that with Tommy and

Laurie now living in the mansion, God's work was going on all night and all day, even on weekends, and she'd never really fit into that world.

"Surely, you see that this is for the best?" Ranny had explained one evening. "I pray that you can see that this is the way life has to be."

A year passed before Chrissy saw the news on the P.L.U.M.B. Christian news show that God had moved Tommy and Laurie to separate. Another six months on, she was not surprised to learn that her Ranny had not married Laurie, while Tommy had gone deep undercover in the sodomite world in hopes of bringing about real change. He'd moved into a Capitol Hill board and bath house thought to be central to their agenda. Tommy was still spending time with Ranny and Laurie on the weekends, however.

That's when Chrissy realized what the signs had been leading to. Since the accident, she hadn't been enough for Ranny, or for any man. No one would or could ever love her again. Ranny had tried to be kind, but her deformed face had driven him to accept a life dedicated only to God, when he could have had so much more.

Now, the declining nature of her home served as a constant reminder of how she had been cheated. Every moment on this Earth was a reminder of her deep pain. Everything was a reminder of the pain. But this was May, the one time of each year when she could almost feel good about her life.

She could feel like she was making a difference now. The bedazzling was a reminder of that in the small space between her bed and desk she would figure out how to make a difference, just as she had every year for ever so long now.

In this tiny piece of a huge ugly world, she was safe and protected and everything was beautiful. Chrissy pulled a sheer pink robe over her pink satin nightie, slipped her feet into pink slippers. She leaned down and found the locker in which she kept her May work bag, retrieved the key from its magnetized case on the bed rail and opened the box.

As was the case every year, when she opened the box, the memories came pouring out. Such memories. All her girls, all helped, all in a better place now. She had done that, and beamed as she thought about it.

For now, she didn't need much, just the red notebook.

She flipped it open to the list as she turned on her computer. Waiting for the computer to load, she looked at the list. Carol, of course, from just a year ago. But also Debby and Susanne and Sophie and Lindsay and… well, nine in all. This year would make 10. That was something to be proud of.

So few people stuck with the efforts to make the world a better place. Chrissy wasn't like those others. She persevered. Ten was a nice round number. She wondered if maybe this wouldn't make a nice time to stop. She giggled at that thought.

"Every year I think maybe I've done enough, but every year I know I have to keep going," she thought. "I can't stop. My girls need me. Besides, what else would I do with my time?"

Chrissy spent most of her year as a cleaning supplies representative. She also liked that, making the world a cleaner place was a good thing. But May was her month. It had all ended for her,

really, on May 18 so many years back.

It hadn't seemed like an ending at the time, it had seemed like a beginning. Getting crowned Miss Garden State had seemed like the beginning of so much that would come.

She knew better now. Later, when she'd realized it and started helping her girls, she realized May 18th only made sense. She looked at the list, and thought that since Sandra, her first, she hadn't helped out anyone from the Miss Teen contest.

"That's a shame," she thought. "Especially since there are really 50 contests, it's almost unfair. I should close out my first 10 the way I started it."

The computer was working now. Her first course of action, as she did every time she logged in, was to go to her "booty search" file. She kept a couple lists of stories dealing with pageant winners, and the automatic notifications of everything from Miss USA to Pork Queen or Lobster Queen could pile up if she wasn't on top of them.

This batch had another six newly crowned queens. Really, there was too much work that needed to be done.

"But just me to do it," she sighed.

She cut and pasted the details on each of the new notifications into booty search. "Impressive," she thought, "this year ends with 326 girls. All of them now basking in the glory of their beauty. None of them knowing they're standing on the edge of a precipice. Only one will be lucky enough to be saved from what is coming. Who…"

The files each included the data on the girls and, of course, photo. She scanned the entire list, smiling back at the beauty queens, her sisters, though now more like her daughters. She didn't like the sound of that. Part of the pain was discovering that there was no real love in this life once your natural glory faded. She sighed. This lack of love was tragic. Still, Chrissy thought, look at her. Daughters was a bit much. Maybe more like younger sisters, from Dad's second marriage to a young model. That made more sense.

"Down to business," she thought. Chrissy was always organized, but combing through the list was always more art than math. A quick search gave her a full list of Miss Teen state winners. On one level, they were all worthy. They were all young and beautiful. But she went from photo to photo, enlarging the photos to the point just before they started to pixelate to see who really spoke to her. Who had Chrissy's spark?

Within two hours, she had the list down to three. Candy Johnson of Pineville, Oregon. Jessica Roberts of Kingdom City, Missouri. Nev Sparrow, of Chances, Colorado.

There wasn't much to choose from among these three lovely young girls. Their eyes, all hazel, all had a charming sparkle. Their smiles were yummy. Their cheeks just begged to be held. Their hair, well, almost identical and Chrissy very much approved.

Nev worried her, a bit, though.

"Look at that, 5'6" and 136 pounds? That's 20 pounds too much for her frame. It's fine for now, but she's just barely hanging on, isn't she? That will catch up to her far too quickly…

"Oh dear. Oh, poor dear."

She smiled and used her right index finger to trace along the young girl's face in the photo.

"I think so," she finally said. She flipped her notebook to page one, and for the 10th time circled May 18th. "Let's sat 9:30 p.m., if that works for you, Nev Sparrow of Chances, Colorado. Poor girl. Don't worry, I'm coming."

Chapter 15

May 18 6:55 a.m.

The camper van was peppy today. Coach thought that wasn't really much of a surprise. It was carrying a much lighter load than normal.

His perfect boy was complete, so he'd moved him down to his coaching chamber, the room behind the false wall in his basement. It was a hell of a place. Nothing down there to distract a man from what mattered in life, molding young bodies to perfection. The room was built around the primary honorees, of course. One was now in place, humming slightly. The other was in the back, and she was just about done, just about ready to join her partner in perfection.

This was an exciting couple days facing him. Coach had just finished the last practice of the year, after state championships, which sadly hadn't included any of his current crop of kids. They worked hard, Coach knew. They just didn't have it.

Most years, he would be disappointed, crushed, not to have a single boy or girl make it to the state finals. It was the sort of thing that could cause him to lock himself in the chamber for days and pour over the films he'd made of his coaching to look for flaws, search for ways in which he could do a better job.

But that was most years, not this year. Right now, in this van, heading north towards Salina where he'd turn west, Coach knew he was on the verge of greatness. Everything he'd planned for, everything he had dreamed of, was about to come to a close, a victorious close.

This was no time to celebrate, of course. Who could forget the football players who got so excited at being free and clear that they spiked the ball on the three-yard line? Without discipline, without the will to follow through and keep giving everything you had until the final whistle, touchdowns became fumbles, gold medals became "also rans" and the best of a generation became not quite good enough.

"Van Gogh didn't stop until the ear was off," he liked to remind his athletes. "Sacrifice is required for greatness."

This was what kept Coach going right now. He was so close. After the better part of a decade, he was on the verge of victory. He just had to keep his head down and keep his legs moving. The victory dance could wait.

He had it planned out. The drive, strictly obeying speed limits and stopping every two hours for 60 jumping jacks and some stretching, would take 10 hours and 25 minutes. He'd have to plan on at least three fill-ups, two to get there and one before he met the athlete because right after was not a good time to stop for gas. He'd had a good night's sleep, but would need to make sure he fueled himself up properly. He would want to carb load at breakfast, then focus on protein and finally sugar for energy. So, the plan was to arrive in Chances around 9 p.m. and get to the house at 9:25 p.m.

Once more, he mentally sifted through the scouting reports. She was a good one. Nicely focused. Three years all state, one year as schoolgirl prep athlete of the year for Colorado, and an All-America medal thrown in for good measure.

He'd felt a little odd focusing on a soccer player. He'd always believed in the Tom Landry, Gil Brandt philosophy, always go for the best athlete. A good coach can fit help them become the perfect piece of their puzzle, but great athletes are great athletes. Still, he didn't like the fact that he'd passed over soccer to this point. Coach admired athletics, at all levels and in all ways. What matters most is that someone is in the game. Which game doesn't matter so much.

More than that, he was down to the end. He wasn't drafting in a general sense, he was drafting to fill a specific need. This girl had a killer cross. He'd seen her send balls in to her teammates, hit on a straight line, bending down just perfectly, from 40 yards.

"Hell of a left leg on you, Nev," he said to himself, with a proud chuckle. "Perfect. Just perfect."

Chapter 16

May 18 2:01 p.m.

It hadn't just been the beauty pageant victims that had convinced Agent (in training) Sparrow to get out of the office and catch the flight he'd booked. There was nothing concrete. There wouldn't be.

And it was still a million to one shot against. Really it was three million to one shots. While he'd studied enough statistics to know that Nev's odds hadn't just increased by two-thirds. Three one in a million longshots don't mean the odds are now one in 333,333 (which remained pretty good odds for his sister). The odds remained one in a million, three different times.

Still, here he was, in a cab, zooming past monuments that still thrilled him, on his way to Reagan National Airport. Really, it was embarrassing. He was staring at the maps he'd made, and looking at records of past murders and disappearances, and all he could think of was Nev's voice. All he could picture was his little sister, home alone, and one of these maniacs showing up at her door.

So he'd run outside the FBI building and caught a cab, and if there wasn't too much traffic and the security lines weren't too long, he'd be on a plane to Denver within the next 90 minutes. That would be good enough, with the drive, to get him home by … say 7:30 p.m. with the time difference. Assuming there were no delays, and the car he'd rented (and forgot to cancel) was still available.

He'd decided against the trip this morning, so right now he didn't have his bag with him. He didn't have a toothbrush or a razor or, well anything. Of course, it was home, and Mom always kept a closet shelf with extra toothbrushes and disposable razors, in among the shampoos and soaps and deodorants. She still bought his favorites, or what had been his favorites when he was a kid. He was pretty sure there were even a few items he'd left behind when he'd left home for good after college. They wouldn't be stylish, but sweats were sweats.

He could deal with just sweats. Reading through the cases had given him a bad feeling. Getting rid of that pit of the stomach unease would be worth arriving at home with only a backpack into which he'd stuffed an armload of files.

The files were, frankly, amazing. One of the central problems with working bizarre serial killer cases was turning out to be that the experience was both seriously creepy and way too much fun. The too much fun side of the equation was why he'd made the decision to postpone the trip home.

His agent hadn't insisted. Brody wasn't so sure his agent was really that interested in what he was working on. There were other threads that needed following, and he was working those. Brody, really, was working on background.

"Wow, though," he thought. "Interesting background."

He'd separated the files, and each pile took up an entire table on the basement room they were using at the headquarters in downtown D.C. They could have been working out of Quantico, but truth be told, nobody who doesn't live in rural Virginia likes working at Quantico. Place was a pain in the ass by mass transit, for one.

He'd had the room to himself for a couple days. That actually made quite a bit of difference. No one was around to tell him to clean up his shit. In this case, that had helped. Staring at the separate piles, while digging through file after file, had focused him. That focus had allowed him to see the three piles clearly.

But really it was after talking with Nev that the pennies started dropping. He'd looked down at the ticket he wasn't using and noted the date, May 18. And it had hit him that the beauty queen pile had some similar dates. The initial report on one May 19. Three were first reported on May 20. One was reported on May 22 and four were reported later than that. But inside the reports, the times of death indicated, well, nothing exact. But they could all have been killed at the same day. Given the state of the body found on May 19, that date would have to have been before May 19. May 18, today, was a likely candidate. Every year, on May 18. For nine years.

And this was a serial killer, and they were freaks and often obsessive compulsive, at least about their victims. Serial killers had amazingly set modus operandi and, well that meant today. The oldest case had been a Miss Teen. None of the others had been, but this was 10 and that was a nice round number and maybe that was a bit off the charts guesswork, but, Nev was a Miss Teen.

So he'd kind of panicked.

And while panicking he'd looked at the push pin map he'd made of the disappearing athletes. What hit him was what wasn't in that set. Not one of the athletes was from Colorado, and not one was a soccer player. True, there were more states without pins in them than with pins. There were also other sports that young people played that

96

weren't on the list, at least he thought there were. Rugby? Do they play that in high school? Lacrosse? He wasn't sure. And the third one, the unknown targeting smart kids, several of those kids had been recognized for their work on Lincoln. Nev had been recognized for her work on Lincoln.

In his head, an argument went back and forth:

"It's a long way from hard evidence."

"But Nev is our little sister and she's all alone."

"That doesn't make her a target. This is beyond circumstantial, into random coincidence."

"But she's our little sister, and she's all alone."

"I know she's all alone, so I'm inflating the importance of connections."

"But she's our little sister, and she's all alone."

Every time he repeated that in his head, he'd felt like it was a bit stronger as a case for getting to Colorado as quickly as possible.

"Jeepers, Nev could be a target of any of these folk," he'd decided. "She's all alone, on an important date, and she could be the target of all of them."

As the cab was making the final loop into the airport he was convinced that while his worst case was over the top, even preposterous, he'd made the right decision.

Not that he'd felt confident enough in his fears to share them. He wasn't stupid. When he'd told his guy this morning that he was going to postpone his days off a little, stay on and work the files, the reaction had been a grunt that seemed to imply "whatever."

Now he called.

"Agent Thomas, I had to leave the office."

"Aren't you already on vacation?"

"No, I delayed that, this morning, remember?"

"Huh."

"But now I realized I have to leave."

"Marinara again?"

"No, I mean, yeah, that, but also, I was thinking of my vacation. My little sister needs me there."

"Oh, fine. You have the time. Enjoy."

Agent Sparrow stopped himself from responding that this wasn't the sort of trip you enjoyed. He stopped himself from blabbing on about his fears. Instead, he just said "Thanks. See you soon."

With that he was in line to check in.

"Am I in time," he asked an attendant, "for the Denver flight?"

"Oh, yes, sir. That's been delayed. You've got an additional two hours. Plenty of time."

He was both relieved to have both made the flight and avoided a mad airport dash, and panicky. He felt a shiver down his spine. The math was pretty basic. That would have him arriving at the family house right around 9:30 p.m.

"I hope that's early enough," he thought, before chastising himself for that. "Of course it's early enough. What difference can a couple hours make?"

He'd get a soda and sit down with the files. That would keep him occupied.

Chapter 17

May 18th 3:45 p.m.

Nev realized her mistake. Never dive into a Criminal Minds marathon when you're home alone.

The early episodes were creepy, the psycho who glued eyelids open so his victims had to look at him, sheesh. The people who write this stuff must be total freaks. Or is this all real? Is this what Bro does all day, track down freaks who glue eyelids open?

On the other hand, it was pretty fun. Scaring yourself half to death in a family home that looks like it came straight from the Hollywood set of just about every slasher movie ever _ Victorian style with the big turrets. Isolated, dark street, with no neighbors for half a block in either direction. Now that she thought about it, even they were both on vacation. Typical slasher film quiet town. And here she was, after her last chat with Bro, now a prime target for as many as three psychos…

"Okay," she thought. "Calm down a bit. A good scare is fun, but let's not go crazy."

She'd scrunched further down under her blanket and adjusted the cushions, and was perfectly comfy in her building fear when the phone rang.

Nev screamed. Then she noted the "Bro" on her screen.

"Jerk," she said, picking up the call.

"Nev, you okay, this is Bro," a reassuring voice told her. "Just letting you know I am on my way. I decided it wasn't fair to leave you alone."

"Jerk."

"What?"

"You scared the crap out of me."

"It's my special skill." It was his special skill when they were younger. Brody would see Nev preparing to leave her room, the house, whatever, and would hide in a darkish spot that would be on her path when she started walking. When she neared, he'd step out and say "boo" and she'd scream. A couple times she fell down. Once, when she was eight, she wet herself (she claimed this wasn't at all fair, as she was on her way to the toilet when he ambushed her). Brody would wait for minutes, sometime as long as 15 minutes, for her to walk into his traps.

After she screamed, they'd both laugh, a lot. Then she'd punch him in the chest and call him a jerk, and he'd say exactly what he said now.

"Just trying to get you ready to face the real world."

"You're still a jerk."

"To be fair, how was I supposed to know a phone call would scare you."

Then he added, "I get in a little later than planned, but will be there tonight."

"I know, leave the light on and door unlocked."

"Maybe lock the door. I can ring the doorbell, but yeah. I will see you tonight, sometime around 9 is my guess."

"I'll order pizza for when you get here!"

"Yeah, but seriously, lock the door."

"In Chances?"

"It's a favor, for me. Just do it to make your big brother happy, okay."

"Lock the door. Check. Any other survival tips until you get here?"

"Great. Just, you know, be careful until I show up. I'm kind of freaked by the stuff I'm working on."

"I'm a big girl, Bro. See you soon, jerk."

But after hanging up, she went up to the main floor locked the front door, then checked the back door. That was always locked. She thought about that, the front door was a big thick oak door with a little old school iron latched peep window. It was locked with a thick dead bolt. Lock that and she was safe.

The back door ... about half window, with a lock she pried open more than a couple times when she'd forgotten her house keys. Hopefully psycho killers don't check for back doors, she joked with herself. Ha.

She went upstairs to her bedroom, which actually had a small ante-chamber that she used as her personal gym. Her room was actually in one of the turrets. The far end was round and all windows.

Just in case, she looked around for a weapon. Something to use in self-defense. Dad had a hunting rifle. She went up the steep stairs to the third floor to check on it. It was inside the black cabinet in her dad's study. But that was a stupid locked steel cabinet. She wondered if the keys would be around somewhere. After poking around in her dad's desk drawers for several minutes, she thought the clear answer was no. "He probably takes those with him," she thought. "A lot of good that does me during an attack."

She thought about that for a second.

"Well, no gun. Just as well. I don't know how to use one."

A kitchen knife, of course, would make sense, but that would be embarrassing when Bro arrived and found her on the couch clutching a kitchen knife under her blanket. It would be doubly embarrassing if she forgot about it while watching Criminal Minds and cut herself during one of her all too common scared jumps. The last thing she wanted was for Brody to arrive and have to run her to the hospital because of a self-inflicted wound.

Rule one of self-defense, she thought, don't injure yourself. Okay, that's a good rule one. What should rule two be? Be prepared, obviously. So what do I have?

Her Miss Teen trophy, hmmm … Huge chunk of acrylic, pointy mountain top and probably weighed two pounds. And she could put it on a basement shelf behind her and say their mom was showing it off if Brody noticed. She picked it up.

Good to get this out of my room, in any case. But she had to admit it was pretty cool looking, two inches thick, and clear until you got to the mountain peak, which wasn't clear to simulate snow. Oh yeah, she thought. I could knock the crap out of someone with this.

She looked at the other trophies on the shelves her dad had built into her bedroom wall. Several could work in a pinch. The Colorado Prep Girl Athlete of the Year one, in particular. But she had a heavy ball that she could throw, she supposed.

And … well, this line of thinking was seriously creeping her out.

Okay, I locked the door as a favor to Bro. He was freaked out because that's a big brother's job, to freak out. Of course, Bro never really got scared. Not getting scared was kind of his thing.

"Wow, I am not going to have a lot of fun tonight thinking this way."

She had her Miss Teen trophy in her hand, so she brought that downstairs with her and half hid it on a shelf.

"Get over it, Nev,' she told herself. "Bro is on his way, and he's the ultimate badass. He's an FBI agent. Can't get much safer than that."

She re-snuggled onto the couch, under the blanket. Enough of this crap, she thought. This is my night. Nothing gets to freak me out unless I decide it should freak me out.

"Getting scared works up an appetite," she said. She unscrewed the top off a Diet Pepsi and chugged enough to wash the grease off her tongue. Then she opened a box of Oatmeal Crème Pies.

A couple clicks on the remote showed her that next up in her night of terror was "Natural Born Killer."

"Good," she thought. "I'll have a lot to talk about with Bro when he gets here. Like, how does he deal with this stuff for real?"

Chapter 18

May 18th 8:21 p.m.

Nev had reached inevitable point in her marathon where she was thinking it might be time to read a book. She jumped up from her couch nest to re-lock all the doors. Then she peaked out the front windows to make sure she was safe. What she'd seen was her deadly dull small town: in the low light, there were a few yellow globes of porch light, her empty street looked totally empty, and behind the street was only the looming shadow of pine trees filtering out the dying rays of sun.

"This is why we subject ourselves to creepy marathons," she thought. "Because real life is so boring."

While she was up, though, she remembered that she'd promised Bro a pizza, and she was craving one herself. Mushrooms and onions, extra cheese, she was thinking. Bro would want meat, and he'd want a lot. She got out her phone, clicked on large and Italian sausage, onion and mushroom, clicked on extra cheese. On special, $18.25. Mom and Dad had left her a stack of cash in the kitchen, figuring she'd need money for groceries, and she should be able to order in a couple times at least. She plucked a $20 bill, and wondered if that covered the tip for the pizza guy. Can $1.75 be enough for delivery? She didn't pay for delivery, ever. That was her Dad's deal, or her Mom's deal, or Bro's deal. Well, the order said it would be here at 9 p.m. Maybe he'd be here by then, or at least call by then. She could ask.

She did hope he was here soon. She knew she would head back downstairs and continue to freak herself out, and she was looking forward to swapping stupid jokes about the marathon with him. That seemed less creepy.

And if Bro was late? Well, he'd show up to find cold pizza. Ha, she thought, that would be pulling out all stops for his welcome home.

Chapter 19

May 18th 8:24 p.m.

The sign read "Chances: 18 miles" so Chrissy decided Cal's Gas and Food Stop was as good a place for a final staging as anywhere. When she'd pulled in both sides of the pump were blocked. A camper van and a small car of some sort. Both drivers appeared to be inside, paying by cash.

She'd be doing the same thing, but she still couldn't help thinking it was a bit rude, to leave their cars blocking the pumps. She had a bit of time, but she was on a schedule.

Before she could get angry, though, one of the drivers came out. Funny man in a tweed jacket who reminded her immediately of a sitcom version of a college professor. "Oh," she realized. "He was paying cash so he had to go inside."

She watched him get into his small car and drive off, slowly. She pulled in behind him and watched his taillights vanish in the dark towards Chances before getting out of her car to fill up.

The camper van across the island from her was humming. Apparently, it was still running while the driver was inside, paying. She noted that the engine wasn't running. It was some kind of generator. It was just a low hum, though.

"That's a smart van," she thought. "Too big for one, but it's nice."

This stage of her missions was always troubling to her. She always stopped about this far from the home of the new girl on the way in to make sure she didn't have to stop on the way out. It made her feel odd, almost as if she was acknowledging that what she was going was wrong. It wasn't, though. She was on a mission of mercy. She was doing God's work. She knew this.

Still, she admitted that not everyone would see her actions in the same light. Paying attention to details like this was one way of ensuring her mission continued.

It wouldn't be a good idea to find out her car was almost on empty as she was leaving, to end up stranded a block away from one of her girls.

The pump clicked off and she took her next smart step. Her mind wandered as she walked toward the building to find the cashier. Always pay cash. If she used a credit card, people might notice she'd been in the area, and had been in the areas nearby all of her girls. If she paid cash, there was no record. There might be a video of her at a gas station, but video records from gas stations 20 miles from her girls wouldn't really help anyone identify her. In the movies, police were always finding clues from random video tapes over which they'd run facial recognition software.

Chrissy didn't think that happened in real life. She paused to think about that. She never really followed up on her girls, what happened with the investigations afterwards. She left her girls in as tidy a setting as she could. But after her mission was complete, it was complete. She never felt the need to retrace her steps.

She came out of her day dream as she was standing in front of the cashier. Behind the cashier she noted the security television monitor, and she smiled for the camera. Still a pretty smile if she turned to her left cheek, she thought.

As she was smiling, she heard a chuckle, and spun around prepared to be offended. It had come from the dining table, where a large, strong and very ruggedly but quite handsome man was staring at her. He gave her a small wave when she looked at him.

"Excuse me?" she said.

"Sorry, Ma'am," he answered. "I just found that endearing. Smiling for the camera."

"I wasn't doing it for your benefit. It was a simple reflex. I see a camera, and I smile. Is that a problem for you?"

But in her head, she was asking herself what was going on. She felt a connection to this stranger.

"Chrissy, are you flirting?" she wondered. "Not the time. Not the place."

Still, she liked the look of his shoulders. He had the presence of a football player about him. And a very strong jaw, like that comic book detective. She had to admit, she hadn't felt any sort of spark with a man for a long while, but there was something about this one. At a different time, in a different place?

"Not at all," the man responded. "It was just a very pretty thing to see. Sorry to interrupt and sorry to bother you. You're on camera quite a lot, then?"

"Polite, handsome and he clearly likes me," she thought.

"I used to be," she said. "It's been a while."

"Well then, anything I'd remember?"

"I certainly hope not."

She realized she was hiding her scars, something she hadn't done in ages. She smiled, a big smile, careful to turn her right side away from him.

"If you don't mind me being forward, Ma'am, that scar just means you've lived," he said. "Don't hide it. It's character. You are very beautiful, and the scar doesn't hurt that."

Chrissy felt tears forming in her eyes. She wasn't sure why. She thought that was such a kind thing to say. "Here, in the middle of nowhere, when I have no time for this, I meet a sensitive man, a sweet man," she thought.

Clearly, this was not a good conversation to engage in. She had to remain focused. She was, after all, on a mission. Her mission wasn't exactly the sort she could share with a stranger, no matter how great the spark. She took her change and excused herself, to splash a little water on her face and get her head straight.

When she came out of the restroom, she avoided the man's eyes.

"Best to leave him to enjoy his cheeseburger," she thought. But she watched him in the window reflection and he was watching her walk away, and smiling.

It had been a long time since she'd been rattled by a man's glance. At least a decade. There was something about him that she found almost irresistible, though. She even sensed a kindred spirit. But that was a crazy thought, and she wasn't crazy. She drove her car away from the pumps to the dark outer edge of the parking lot. Then she turned off the car and stared into the dark of the Colorado countryside.

"Deep breaths, Chrissy," she told herself. "Don't get thrown off your game this easily. Just relax and get back in the zone. Just relax."

She found it an unfortunate coincidence that 15 minutes later, when she was finally ready to get back on course, the man pulled out of the station in his camper van, headed towards Chances, as well.

"Come on, Chrissy. Dear little Nev Sparrow needs us. She needs us now. Let's forget about chance encounters and just get moving."

Chapter 20

May 18th 8:29 p.m.

Coach realized he'd forgotten all about his meal when she walked in. Coach didn't get attracted to women, at least not since he'd started his project. He believed that success requires dedication, and from the moment he started this effort, he'd remained completely devoted.

"Art is 10 percent inspiration, but 90 percent perspiration," was a motto of sorts. He was making art. He was making perfection. His had to be a lonely path.

But what if it didn't? He'd sensed a connection, some deep understanding in her first glance. Was that possible?

Women, teachers back home and single mothers of his athletes, had flirted with him before. But he didn't have time for love, or romance, in his life. Not if he was going to complete what he started. Coach fully intended to finish what he'd started.

Maybe that was it. Maybe it was the fact that tonight he'd be done, he'd have completed what he set out to accomplish so many years ago.

"Man, though, something about those eyes," he thought. It was more than finding her attractive, it had been an actual attraction. Coach could see the same thoughts had been in her eyes. They'd had a moment.

He thought of a James Blunt song, of a woman seen on a subway, a connection made in a single smile. Of course, that song had stated those two would never be together, and that had to be the result here, as well. His heart had raced, he'd daydreamed of taking her hand.

Right now, he couldn't stop his mind from wondering if she wasn't the one who could share his life, his passions. He shook his head, thinking about his project, who would truly get that part of him?

"Odds against that are pretty long," he finally decided. "In any case, she's gone and I'll never see her again. Still, it was nice to feel that way, even if only for a couple minutes. It always pays to take a second and appreciate the beauty life brings."

He finished his cheeseburger, put a $50 bill on the counter to cover gas and dinner, and walked back out to his van. As he was pulling on Highway 40, he noted a smaller car waiting in the dark at the edge of the lot, but didn't give it another thought.

Chapter 21

May 18th 8:39 p.m.

Brody Sparrow hadn't wanted to waste time slowing down to call until after he'd raced through Denver International Airport. They'd actually landed early. Tailwinds, apparently. After getting off the plane, he hadn't thought it would be possible, but he'd gotten to the shuttle bus in less than 15 minutes. The bus was pulling up as he raced toward it with his backpack, and it was gone almost as soon as he was aboard.

He was at rental car outlet in less than 15 minutes.

The car, a small but very functional Hyundai, had been waiting for him. Everything had gone perfectly since he'd landed. He saw that as a sign. Was he meant to get home as fast as possible?

When he'd had the chance to have a bit of a breather, after pulling the car onto the long highway out of the airport, he'd also felt more than a bit foolish. The chances that Nev actually faced any danger tonight were something below minimal. They were so low that he wouldn't dare contact his office, or even local police in Chances. They were so low as to not really be odds, at all.

It was nothing more than a feeling in his gut, a sense that he had to get home as fast as possible. It was a sense that Nev needed him, and needed him now.

His rising panic was simply explained: He was a big brother and had made a promise, and, well, his head was filled these days with horribly grizzly images. He was overreacting.

They were seriously grizzly images, though. So many young people, so many kids. Kids just like Nev. Smart kids, pretty kids, jock kids. He could see the crime photos. So much blood. So much anger and violence.

Brody didn't mind overreacting. He was doing it in the best interests of his sister. He could live with that. So what should he do now? Should he call Agent Carc back in D.C.? How would that conversation go?

"Boss, I'm racing to my family's house as fast as I can, but could you have an agent get there first?"

"Why?"

"A gut feeling."

"Is there something wrong there?"

"Maybe."

"Why maybe?"

"Well, everything was fine a couple hours ago, but, you know, it's a dangerous world…"

Yeah, that conversation wasn't going to end well.

Neither would a call to Chances P.D. Back in the day, two of the guys who were officers now had been friends. But that was then. Now they saw him as a bit high and mighty. Maybe he dropped the FBI into their conversations a bit too much.

They'd never let him live it down if he called now, with nothing to go on.

So panic, but sharing this panic with anyone was pointless. There was nothing to share. There was no point in warning Nev, because there was nothing happening.

"No, this panic is all on me," he was thinking as he pulled into the passing lane. In the dying light of the day, the mountains on his right-hand side were, of course, blood red. But they were most nights, either that or burnt orange. Just keep the mountains to the right and I'll be home in 20 minutes.

Now, as he drove, he ran over the items that had pricked at his brain about the investigation. He could see the map, with its three colors of pins. While he'd been staring at it earlier, he could sense the blank area of the map around Chances was the epicenter of a pattern. Now, thinking about that, he realized that was nonsense. He knew nothing about the methods of these killers. He could only make broad, general guesses about their motivations. Hell, he was only able to be certain about one of his three serial killers actually existing. The other two groups he'd identified hadn't met his bar for classification as the serial work of a single person. Those deaths, and disappearances, were still seen as separate acts. And he admitted, there had been convictions. They weren't all open cases.

He'd dismissed a couple previous arrests because the reports noted that the evidence wasn't strong. But, well, lots of people pursue pretty young women, and athletes were prone to risk taking.

"No," he thought. "I'm not wrong about that side of things."

115

Police missed the connections, and the previous three arrests were mistakes. He had noticed something important, something others had overlooked. The patterns that emerged from the victims were compelling. There were three sets of victims, and there was every indication that these were serial killers who had killed in the past and would continue to kill until caught or stopped.

"That's my job, to stop them before they kill again," he thought. But this line of thinking made him feel a little guilty. "Why am I here, then?"

He knew justice was better served if he'd stayed in the FBI basement working the case. This trip might have been for his planned days off, but wasn't he just mixing up his fixation on this case with his love and concern for his little sister on this journey?

"Okay, the connections to Nev are tenuous. But it's still not a bad thing to get home to see her. She's still my sister, and I'm allowed to worry."

Brody knew his concern was silly, but he stepped down on the gas and his little car lurched towards 80 miles an hour, about its top speed, he thought.

As he sped by Cal's, he checked the dashboard clock. He figured he'd be home right around 9 p.m. He'd made good time. He'd made great time. He really couldn't have been expected to be there any sooner than he would be now.

"Jeesh, calm down," he told himself. "She's all right. Everything is all right."

He tried to push the accelerator a little deeper into the floor. Maybe he should just give her a call to let her know he was almost there, he thought.

Chapter 22

May 18 8:57 p.m.

The Professor pulled his car under the long branches of some tall pines and peered at the address on the house across the street.

"That's it," he told himself. "Nev's house."

He stared at the place. A parochial attempt at Gothic. He left himself starting to sneer and made an effort to stop. "The way the house looks doesn't matter, does it?" he thought. "It's what's inside. It's the setup."

He was looking through the uncovered picture windows. Lights were on in most rooms, meaning he had a great view. He could only get half a peek into the basement, but he could see the blue glow of a television set, and what he was certain was the shadow outline of Nev's head and shoulders in that glow.

"From the only perspective that matters, it looks ideal," he told himself. "Nev is alone. No one else is home. Perfect."

No one was ever home, he thought. This is, after all, a latchkey generation, and that goes double for high performing kids. Absentee parents were a constant blessing and the Professor always marveled at that. High performing parents lead to high performing kids? He wondered.

He suspected that his students were more alone than mediocre kids in other ways, also.

They appeared relatively friendless. Some of them had online friends, of course, if that counts as an actual friend. A couple of his pupils appeared to have had real life friends, at least from the photos on their walls, but they didn't appear to spend much time together, at least in person. He'd never run into anyone other than the student when he showed up for a lesson. That was actually interesting, and he suspected exceptional. Was it the drive to succeed that isolated these young people, or were they driven to succeed because of their isolation? There is an interesting bit of research in that, he thought.

Research aside, looking at Nev's house, he was convinced that once again he had chosen well. The house had long stretches of empty space, or in the parlance of such communities, lawns. Pine trees were particularly good at dampening sound, the waves had to bounce through a maze of needles. In a setting like this, where the tree branches started just a few feet off the ground, and intertwined on four sides of the house (the open street being the lone, treeless, exception), the odds of completing his tutoring uninterrupted were, as always, excellent.

Of course, he had to admit that his students were not the rowdy types. They didn't scream in the manner of jocks and cheerleaders. They led quiet, internal, lives. He noted with some pride that they died the way they lived.

"We are who we are," he thought. "This above all, to thine own self be true. The Bard was rarely wrong. Temet Nosce. Know thyself."

He pulled his cane from the back seat, and twisted the handle while holding the collar. With a slight tug, a long silver blade came out.

Perfect working order. He pushed the blade back in and gave it half a twist then opened the car door, telling himself "Qui docet in doctrina," let the teacher teach, as he pulled himself up from his seat, balanced on his cane. He grabbed his satchel. It was quite large for a briefcase, but his needs were larger than a briefcase could handle. High quality brown leather, a single soft lid that closed with a strong clasp. The shoulder strap made it just manageable. The ropes, the goggles, the plastic suit and gloves, the whole kit, fit into the satchel perfectly.

Before he was halfway across the street, a Ford pickup truck with a bright triangle of a sign proclaiming "Tony's Pizza: We Deliver. 30 minutes or it's free!" had come screeching around a corner towards Nev's house. The Professor was stepping onto her lawn just as the brakes squealed to a stop. The driver quickly opened his door and hopped out, dropped the tailgate and opened a small warming oven in the back. He slid a pizza box out, and The Professor couldn't help but notice the worried look on his face. He looked like a man being hunted. The open front door of the truck was emitting an overwhelming barrage of heavy metal music. The Professor also noted the smell of marijuana mixed with that of the pizzas in the back. Clearly, this young man was of no interest. A mindless drone, a worker bee, a citizen of an ignoble civilization. Necessary for the benefit of others. But the item he was pulling from his truck, that could be a useful prop.

"Excuse me young man, is that for Nev Sparrow?"

119

"Huh? Just says Nev on the ticket, so I guess so. Sorry man, huge hurry…"

"Good. Let me save you the time of running up the steps and waiting for her. I'll pay. How much?"

"Uhm what? That'd be great. Like, say, twenty bucks, if, you know, you want to include a tip?"

"Easily done. I'm her uncle. I've just arrived, so let me take this off your hands. It would make a loving uncle happy to surprise his niece."

"Thanks, man, I was afraid I was late, and I've got another pizza due in five minutes and that's across old 40 on County Line on the outskirts of town."

"Then away with you," The Professor said, having no idea what the young man was talking about, but happy to see him so eager to leave the area, and to leave it in such a state of confusion. "He smiled a bit, wondering how long it would be before natural selection sent this regrettable member of the species speeding into an accident. The thought made him smile a little more broadly. He held out the money.

The driver grabbed then stuffed the $20 bill into his front pocket, and handed over the warm box. The Professor took the box, holding the bottom with his cane until he'd balanced it properly.

Before the Professor was convinced he was ready to walk, the driver was in the car and screeching down the street, the muffled sound of heavy metal trailing after the vehicle, and soon rounding the next corner in a squeal of tires.

"This was a fortuitous meeting," The Professor thought. To date, he'd found that ringing a doorbell had always been enough. Students yearning for a life of letters could see in him a model. Yet, on occasion, other options would present themselves. Most often those options arrived in the form of a wide open door. This time opportunity would knock holding a pizza. Holding a gift was, of course, the perfect front for making an entrance with a new student. If you bear gifts, it's only natural that others let fall their guard. Gifts excite us.

The lesson of Troy, of course, was obvious here: Perhaps a bit of "qui totum vult totum perdit," he who wants everything loses everything, was at play? To focus on the material world is to lose our ethereal grasp on the celestial? Perhaps that was a bit unfair, he thought. This gift was, after all, sustenance, even if it was a mound of melted cheese and dough. Could he rightly criticize a young student for lacking a refined palate?

A lesser man, a less fair man, would, perhaps, he reasoned. But this order of a meal would be a free pass for young Nev, at least on this night. What mattered most tonight was not what she wanted to consume, but how her mind worked. He was quite excited to learn. It was always a thrill to meet a new student. He never could stop himself from smiling at this moment. It was, unquestionably, a happy time in life, this liminal phase.

The Professor strode confidently up the sidewalk. If there had been an observer, they might have noted that he almost pranced up the front steps.

"Now it's time for the professor to meet the promising pupil, and determine if her promise has any substance, or is all style," he thought, as he reached for the doorbell with the hand gripping his cane.

Chapter 23

May 18th 8:59 p.m.

Brody could see the lights of Chances just ahead. In a minute or so, state highway 40 would cross County Line and he'd pass into the north side of town.

"Thank god," he thought. "About time this crap is over."

He felt around on the passenger seat until he found his phone. Brody had rules about this. He didn't dial numbers while driving. He'd seen the tests being performed while studying criminal justice as an undergrad, and he'd read case files while completing his law degree before he joined the FBI.

Texting, of course, is insanely dangerous. Everyone thinks they text quickly, but they don't. Even a fast text can take your eye off the road for 20 seconds, and a lot can change on the road in 20 seconds. But Brody didn't limit himself to a no text policy. Dialing a phone could be just as tricky.

The problem starts with the way we see. Human eyes are better than computer eyes because the human brain is insanely flexible. The human eye only actually takes in a fraction of the information that a computerized eye does, but the human brain can instantly analyze that smaller data set in millions of ways. The problem with that is that a lot of what we see is simply filled in by the brain based on expectations.

That's usually fine, but when the brain is being asked to focus on something else, like the phone, it tends to fill in a bit more. What we're seeing is less what's actually there and more what our brain is telling us should be there.

But in this case, in his old hometown, on a road that seemed pretty quiet, he was happy to break his policy.

The phone made Nev scream, for the second time today. The timing was perfect, she thought. This shit is scary.

"Nev, you okay?"

"I am fine, Bro. You getting here soon? I've got pizza coming any moment now."

Brody could feel his body relaxing. After a day of torturing himself, and a couple weeks immersed within the world of psychotic killers, nothing sounded better or more normal than pizza with Nev, sitting and chatting on the couch and maybe keeping the television on as a backdrop to the conversation.

"I can see Chances, sis. I can't be more than a couple minutes away."

"Oh, that's great. It'll be fun."

"You're not kidding. I gotta tell you, I've been freaking out since I left the office today. I know it's stupid, but I've been worried..."

"That's sweet, but I'm a big girl. I could have taken care of myself. I'm glad you're coming, but I didn't need you for protection."

"I know, but I worry."

"About me? Hey, I'm a badass."

Brody laughed, and Nev laughed, until she interrupted.

"Excuse me, Bro. That was the doorbell. Pizza is here. Let me run up and get it."

"Cool."

Nev didn't hang up, though. Brody could hear her clumping up the steps, opening the basement door, shouting "be right there." Then he heard a light "thunk" that he figured was probably Nev placing her phone down on the small table Mom and Dad placed next to the front door for just such situations, when you were about to open the front door with hands full.

Brody reflected on the sounds. It was calming, really. He was a passenger in a little piece of his sister's life. It had been months since he'd seen her. It would be good to catch up.

"She's a good sister," he was thinking when he heard her unlatch the door and the slight creak of its hinges as it swung open.

"Hi, is that for me," he heard her say.

Then he heard a man's voice say, "You are Nev Sparrow?"

"Yep, how much do I owe you?" he heard her ask, then mumble, "Yum, it's hot."

"For the pizza, let's call that my treat," Brody heard the man reply. "But for an abominable paper on the psychological makeup of our 16th president, I'm afraid the tax is much higher. At the very least, you owe me an apology, but we will see."

124

Brody then heard the sound of metal scraping on metal, and immediately the sound of Nev screaming.

Brody screamed "Nev" into the phone, but heard only a loud grunt, a shout of bastard, and what was probably the small table crashing to the floor before the line went dead.

Brody couldn't take his eyes off the phone. "No dammit, dammit," he yelled at the steering wheel, once again flooring the accelerator. "Think, think. Police. 911."

His eyes searched the phone's surface for the phone keypad button. Later, that would be what the police determined had kept him from noticing he was running a red light on the edge of town, at the intersection of County Line and 40.

Brody clicked open the keypad and had just dialed "9 and 1" when the scream of brakes ripped his eyes off his phone. He turned his head just in time to see a Ford pickup with an odd lit up triangle on top tear into the driver side of his little rental car.

He remembered the first flip as the car rolled down County Line. He could see the lights of his small hometown turn upside down. He could almost see the turn off to his old house. He felt as he was spinning towards impact on the roof that he could almost reach out and help Nev. He shouted "Nev" as he was spinning. He would remember that, though that would be the last thing he remembered.

He remembered the initial impact that sent his head cracking against the driver's window, which crumpled under the force. He didn't remember the way his head then bounced from the steering wheel to the headrest and back to the shattered window. He didn't remember the phone slipping from his unconscious hand as the car wrenched side over side yet again. He didn't remember finally coming to rest hanging in his seatbelt, skidding into a curb on the roof of the car.

And he wouldn't know until much later that the driver of the Tony's Pizza truck spun into a light post at an estimated 70 mph after T-boning Brody's vehicle.

Chapter 24

May 18th 9:04p.m.

Nev was having a hard time processing exactly what was going on.

First, the door-bell rang. Nothing strange there. Then she opened the door and an old guy in a tweed jacket with an oversized satchel and a cane was standing under the porch light.

But he was holding a pizza, so normal enough. He asked if the pizza was for her, which was odd enough, but again, he was an old guy, and when she'd taken the box it was reassuringly warm.

Then he'd said no charge, which was really odd, but never turn down a free pizza. She was pretty sure that was one of the rules of life. It might even be a biblical commandment. Nev thought that if not, it should be.

After handing over the box, the man starting talking and coming out of her mini daydream, she realized it was some crap about her Lincoln paper. This was truly weird. "How has a pizza man heard about my paper?" she wondered.

So, she said it out loud.

"How have you heard about my paper? Are you some kind of creep of a pizza delivery guy?"

And, well, it got a lot more bizarre after that.

He'd handed over the pizza, so his hands were free. Suddenly she saw him twisting at the top of his cane. Before she had time to react or even fully form a "What the hell" thought, his right hand had twisted the top off his cane and was drawing out a long blade.

"What the hell," she finally said.

Was that a sword? A sword cane? I thought those were only in movies? A pizza guy seriously has a sword-cane? Who has a sword-cane? Who had either a sword or a cane? Okay, she knew that one. Lots of people had canes. Swords, not so much, though. King Arthur? Robin Hood, though she thought that might actually be a bow and arrow. Still, old pizza guys?

She heard him speaking: "I was impressed, at times, by your study on megalomania and leadership from Caesars through U.S. Presidents. Though I think you made a couple foolish logical leaps in the conclusion."

And then he lunged forward trying to stab her with his sword. The little table holding her phone went flying as she dodged. Out of the corner of her eye, she saw her phone smash against the floor and pop apart. "Bastard," she shouted.

Nev had to thank God he was a dorky, slow, old guy. Her initial reaction wasn't overly effective. But she figured she'd dodged his initial thrust.

Crap, not completely. As he was stumbling forward having missed her with his sword, the blade fell and had nicked her left leg.

"Bastard," she yelled, and she meant it. He'd cut her. With a goddamn sword? "Fuck you," she added.

He unwisely, she thought, tried a second thrust with his sword. She realized she was still holding on to the pizza box and slammed it onto the blade, using it as a shield. It wasn't a very good shield, though. Obviously, it was a cardboard one. She'd read that Samurai used paper-Mache armor and shields, but only after they stopped being fighters and became accountants or poets. That was a weird thought to have right now, she acknowledged.

Still, while a cardboard pizza box didn't stop a sword (and it had somehow cut her so appeared to be really sharp), between the top of the box, bottom of the box, and the cheese and dough and sauce in between, it did momentarily catch the blade. She was able to twist the sword, then shove it up and back. It wasn't enough of a defense to overwhelm her attacker, but it didn't need to be.

All Nev really needed at this point in her evening was for this freak to be thrown a bit off balance. All she was trying to do was shake him a bit and give herself an opening to counter attack. She set her legs solidly. Dang, that hurts. Stupid sword. Stupid cut.

In that sense, the pizza shield worked perfectly. The old guy half stumbled, and Nev used that half pause to slam her left foot into the guys balls. She was proud of her left foot. She could send a ball a good 40 yards, low and hard and dipping, with that foot. She made pretty good contact here. Not perfect, but as she knew from playing, the look in the old guy's eyes meant she now had the upper hand.

She loved that look of panic in the eyes of someone she was playing against. It meant she'd won. This was a better feeling, because this asshole had stabbed her and was trying to stab her again.

Her mind was racing. "Who the hell is this? Do I know this asshole?"

A solid foot to the groin meant the old guy was now doubling over, looking to be in a lot pain, and really unable to move, at least unable to move very quickly. From Nev's perspective, he'd fallen in an inconvenient spot, straight into the doorway. She would have much preferred if he'd fallen on the porch, or better yet, backwards down the stoop steps. But falling into the front doorway meant he was in the path of the front door. Nev's front door was a solid piece of wood and iron.

He was still gripping the swordcane handle, but it was more prop than weapon at this moment, as he didn't appear able to do much at all, beyond moan in pain. Still, it was sharp and pointy, and she didn't want to even accidentally get cut by it, so she lightly hopped back, then grabbed the thick door in her left hand and slammed it shut as hard as she could.

It wouldn't shut, of course, because the old guy was in the way. But it did make a satisfying crack as it smashed his chest against the doorframe. She could hear the air leaving his lungs, and the gasping after that made her smile.

She was a bit impressed with her reactions. In the television shows, the girls always panicked, cried then died when someone attacked them. "Screw that," she thought.

Nev thought that later would be the time to get creeped and scared and to cry. She had to focus right now.

The movies theme popped back into her head, though. What did the victims always do wrong? They underestimated their opponent. "Okay, then what next?"

At the moment, he was clearly on the floor, and didn't look as if he'd be hopping up quickly. He looked to be in quite a lot of pain, more pain than she was feeling, in fact.

Nev knew it was always after the pain started setting in, when your opponent can't suck in air well enough to keep them working efficiently, that you could do the most damage. In a game, you always initiate contact, and turn on the jets when you caught your opponent wheezing.

"Okay, so how does that apply here," she wondered. She took a second to look around her. The little table was on the floor near her foot. Nice, she thought.

She grabbed a leg. Tested the top and it was still solid. She swung the leg over her head and smashed it towards the guy's hand, the one clutching the sword.

He wasn't quite as out of it as she'd hoped, though. He'd twisted the sword up and the wood of the table was now sticking on the end of the blade. Not the pops and cracks in his hand that she'd hoped for, but not the worst outcome. The blade tip looked to be embedded pretty solidly, so it wasn't useable, at least not now, and for a minute or two.

Still, Nev had seen enough horror movies to know it wasn't over. "What next, what next?" she wondered aloud. "What would the victim do wrong at this point?"

A primary mistake, repeated by pretty much everyone, was to leave the weapon.

She thought about that one. The weapon, for now at least, was not really part of the game. She could try to smash the sole of her right shoe onto the flat of the blade, or his hand, and try to break it free. But the sword was really sharp, and it wasn't just the point that was the problem.

The whole thing was a bit too cutty for her liking.

Even on the floor, looking up at her with glassy eyes ("Is he dazed, or is he crying?" she wondered), he hung on to the blade. She could try to yank it away from him by grabbing the table and pulling back hard. She was pretty sure she was stronger than he was. But that could misfire. That could misfire horribly. She might end up with the table and he with the sword. And, as she knew from the blood trickling down her jeans, that stupid sword was nasty.

"Okay, now what?" she thought as she backed a step away. That was obvious. Every victim, in every movie ever, made the mistake of leaving the bad guy alive. The answer was obvious. "I should kill him."

How, use the mirror to smash his skull open? Run into the kitchen to grab a knife?

She had to bend over, hands on knees, and breath slowly and deeply to keep from retching at that thought. "Oh my God, no. No way."

"Whatever the movie reality might be, I'm not going kill him, even if he is a psycho. I know I can't do that. Fine, he was going to do that to me, but ewwww. And I'm better than that."

In that moment, Nev knew she could not be a cold-blooded killer. She could fight back. She could fight like hell. She could cause pain to stop someone from hurting her. She could get crazy angry. But she would stop short of murder. She had to stop short of murder.

Nev noticed that he was now smiling at her, and starting to move. Which made her jump, and scream a little. But it also gave her a comforting thought. Bro was on his way. In any case, this asshole was now struggling to get to his knees, so she had a head start. And her brother would show up any minute.

"I guess I should call the police," she finally realized. She looked around for her phone. The pieces were pretty much where she would have guessed they would land after the table was knocked over. She looked at the pieces, wondering if she snapped it all back together would it work? Maybe, but maybe there was reason to be in a hurry and she should make that call to the police as soon as possible. Crap, landline. Maybe this is why her mom and dad still had a landline. They always talked about, in case of emergencies. Crap, I hate it when they're right.

She complained about it. A lot. But where exactly was it now. Of course, she'd hidden the stupid thing. Where? Where had she put it? Someplace it wouldn't annoy her. So where was that?

She looked at the odd man in tweed, who was doing little more than moaning and struggling to stand in her doorway.

Okay, I've wasted enough time. She'd seen the movies, this jerk might look incapacitated right now, but it wouldn't be long before he was on his feet and trying to kill her.

How weird that he looks like a professor, she thought as she hurried upstairs to find the phone.

"Maybe he won't be moving for a while," she hoped. "Surely Bro will be here any minute."

Chapter 25

May 18th 9:23 p.m.

The entire faculty at Yardton University had gathered in the oak and cherry wood splendor of the Granville Hall auditorium. It was, without doubt, one of the world's most cultured spots. And as the rows of seats filled with line after line of the world's most brilliant men and women, each considered to rank among the three greatest minds in their area of expertise, or at least thereabouts, the crowd was sending out the murmur reserved for the most solemn of moments.

There was chatter, but it was a low and respectful, and all eyes remained on the stage, where The Professor was seated in the center of a semi-circle made up of the Yardton Chancellor, the university President, and the esteemed heads of the history and political science departments. It was a perfect image, but something was wrong. The Professor could sense something was deeply wrong, though he couldn't imagine what.

There was a polite round of applause building. The dignitaries on the stage all tilted their heads towards him. He tried to stand, but the pain shooting up his legs was overwhelming. The Professor forced himself to stand despite the pain, but as he did he felt the pain race up his arms and engulf his head, and he stumbled forward.

The Professor looked out at what had been an adoring audience of his peers, but he could see in their eyes that they sensed weakness. They were turning against him.

Knowing he would lose them soon, The Professor began to speak, "Astra inclinant, sed non obligant," he began. "The stars may be against us, but they do not define us."

Yet he knew his voice sounded injured and small. From the back of the hall came the first boos, quickly followed by catcalls. He heard "bono malum superate" that good overcomes evil in a single voice, but soon others took up the call. It wasn't long before the first tomato came screaming from the crowd.

The Professor had to dodge, and that caused him to wince. He was left shouting his contemptus saeculi, contempt for these times, but was gaining no traction.

"Fraud," he heard.

"Unoriginal," he heard.

"Mediocrity," he heard.

He staggered to the front of the stage, wanting to destroy those in front of him. But the pain in his legs, in his arms, in his chest was too great. Everything he wanted from life, everything he knew he deserved and had earned, was vanishing into the distance. He tried to reach out and grab it, to hold his promised future tight, but it squirmed out of his embrace.

He looked back, and realized he had been abandoned. The stage was now his alone, and he had been locked onto it. More and more tomatoes splattered around his feet, while lettuce heads bounced off his and somehow increased his pain.

But the vegetables, the humiliation of being turned on by his peers, weren't the worst that was happening. Flaming balls were flying from all directions. As one bounced off the stage, he could see that it wasn't a ball, but a copy of his great work.

"They're burning by work," he thought in horror. "Even my legacy is now disappearing?"

He wanted to scream, to launch himself into his audience and tear them to pieces. "Aut neca aut necare, kill or be killed," he thought. Now, I must act now or it will be too late. I will be forgotten. My work will be forgotten. Even my great mind will be forgotten, and it will be as if I never existed. Act now, act now you fool."

It was these last words that jarred him from his unconscious stupor back to life. As he fully came back to his senses, he looked around. He was stuck in a doorway. The only sounds seemed to be hurried footsteps heading up the nearby steps. He could just see the feet disappearing out of view from around the door.

The pain from his fevered dream, however, that was real. He'd never experienced such pain. Memories of what had happened came back to him. It was a pupil, a student, who had left him like this.

"I stabbed her, she bled," he thought. "That's always when they start screaming and crying and begging for mercy. This one didn't even seem to mind so much."

This had never happened before. She didn't submit to his will so much as impose hers upon him. This was new. This was frightening, but it was also exciting. His students had been meek and timid and not much for the physical side of life. He had often thought of this as a failing on their part, yet another reason they would never truly succeed in the academic world.

He tried to remember a single plea. There hadn't been on. She had yelled something, something obscene if he recalled. But that had seemed as more of a modern battle cry than a plea or lament.

This one, this Nev Sparrow, she apparently was different. She had been vicious in attack, and quick in defense. Was this a sign, he wondered? Was this the world's way of telling him that his time had passed, and he should now forget his lessons?

No, he had been brought to this door by all that he held dear and holy, by academia, by art and letters. He had started this lesson. His finger had moved, and writ upon this page. It was now time to complete this thought, carry on with this lesson.

His world, of letters and ideas, never promised an easy path. Indeed, it promised difficulty and struggle. But the obstacles that presented themselves always led to the most rewarding conclusions. He remembered the pain of the stagnation with his great work. He had been stuck and hopeless, but he had pushed through, and pushed through to greatness.

This was another time when he was being called upon to show that he could be great, that he was worthy of this noble mission. His head was clear now, he knew this to be true.

"For what is the worth of human life, unless it is woven into the life of our ancestors by the records of history?" he muttered to himself, quoting Marcus Tullius Cicero.

His eyes were open. He pulled his legs under him, pushing his back up with arms that had never known such pain. Now fully awake, he remembered the words from his daydream: "Aut neca aut necare, kill or be killed," he said aloud in a determined voice.

First, of course, he had to administer a test. This one was interesting. He paused to consider, and realized she was also significantly more attractive than he was used to. Perhaps something as base as physical appearance had thrown him off his game? He had to admit, she was intriguing. Had there been a twinkle in her eye when she'd first opened the door? He found himself trying to picture her curves, though immediately stopped that train of thought.

"Duty first," he said to himself, though he had to admit that it was disappointing to realize she had shaken him to the point that he'd said it to himself in simple English, and not the Latin "Primum Officium." How deeply did she damage me, he wondered.

The professor pushed himself to a standing position, and found that he could walk.

"My cane," he thought. "Is a bit of a problem."

He tried shaking it free but it was stuck pretty firmly in the wood. He placed a foot on the wood and pulled, using his back. His body ached to the point that he thought he was going to faint, and fail, when suddenly like a cork on shaken champagne, it was free. The suddenness had caught him by surprise, and he stumbled back into the wall and found himself again on the floor. But he had the sword in his hand and he still had his satchel around his shoulder, so all was well.

From the floor, he looked around at his surroundings. Back, beyond the staircase, he could see a kitchen. A kitchen meant knives. He hobbled across the living room and into the kitchen, lurching towards a butcher block. It was full, meaning he didn't have to worry about her being armed at this point. Good thing, he thought, these are cultured blades, as he pulled out a cleaver, and noted the gleaming folds of hardened steel. Damascus steel, a well made weapon, he thought. "Just in case," he thought. "I should take this along for backup."

Now walking better, stronger, with each step, he returned to the steps, and holding his sword and his cleaver, started to climb.

"Aut neca aut necare, kill or be killed," he said again, with a strong sense of the savagery building in his chest. Then added, "But first, duty. This student has a lesson or two to learn tonight."

Chapter 26

May 18 9:30 p.m.

Chrissy felt a tear of pride welling in her eye when she looked across the street at the front door of her new girl's house.

Here it was, after dark and despite the stream of daily news reports of robbers and rapists, this young woman's door was wide open. That's what makes this country, great, she thought. The optimism, the belief in our fellow man, the trust we have in our community.

138

Her thoughts were forming the sort of speech she'd heard hundreds of times from hundreds of pageant contestants. She'd also heard decades of jokes and late-night television monologues and parodies of those speeches. The speeches were shallow, or insincere and wildly out of touch with actual American life. But looking at that open front door was as sure a sign as Chrissy could have asked for that she'd been right, and her girls and all their kindred spirits had always been right.

This was a place where we could trust our neighbor, and strangers didn't have to be threats. This was a nation where a closed door just meant you were shutting out a new friend. It was a beautiful thought, and as Chrissy stepped out of her car then leaned back in to grab her work bag, she was proud to see this evidence at the home of one of her girls. It was speaking to her, don't sneak around the back, just come on in the front door.

The smile on her face faded a bit as she neared the house, however. From the sidewalk leading to the steps, it was obvious the front room was a mess. "Never leave a mess like this, Nev," Chrissy was thinking as she neared the house. But as Chrissy climbed the steps, she said "Oh" aloud.

It was clear from a single glance that the room was in a state because of a tussle of some sort. Chrissy noted a smear of blood near the bottom of the open front door. "Ow," she thought. "That looks like it was slammed on somebody. Ouch."

Chrissy had just stepped into the doorway when she heard a young woman's scream. She froze and looked around. She listened. "Thump, thump, thump, grunt, bastard, thump, thump" was coming from above her head.

She realized no one else was coming into the room she was now standing in, and that there didn't appear to be more than two sets of thumps coming from above.

"This is odd," she thought, as she heard a "thump, crash, thump" followed by what sounded like a car door closing. Chrissy could only think of a couple possible explanations for what was now going on.

These possible explanations were all guesses, she admitted, because this was a totally new experience. She was not unaccustomed to running and thumping and screaming in the houses where she visited her girls. But up to this visit, she had always been involved in the noises. She'd never before been a bystander.

Chrissy thought hard.

It could be that Nev has a boyfriend, or at least an admirer, over and, well, things have gotten a bit out of hand. Or it could be that Nev's parents were arguing rather aggressively, either with each other or with Nev.

Or...well, Chrissy had no idea what else it might be. Assuming the sounds were from Nev, and that Nev was actually upstairs, could Nev be in trouble? Could Nev be under threat? That seemed unlikely. After all, in a strict interpretation of their relationship, Chrissy had to admit that she would be considered the threat to little Nev.

On the other hand, Chrissy had to note, if that was Nev upstairs, Nev didn't seem to be only person screaming. Without seeing it was impossible to know, but it sounded as if Nev was giving as good as she was getting.

She paused and thought deeply on this matter. She was concentrating so intensely that she failed to hear the heavy footsteps coming up the walkway that was now behind her, and then on the floorboards and getting very near.

In fact, Chrissy was so lost in thought that it wasn't until a gruff but pleasant voice, apparently from just a foot or two behind her, asked "Are you Nev Sparrow?"

Chrissy almost jumped out of her skin. She did jump a full three feet forward, and probably two feet high, from the shock.

She realized as she was jumping, while screaming and turning in the air to see who was addressing her, that it was a good thing she'd jumped, because a black handbag appeared to be slicing through the air where her head had been just a second ago.

140

The man attached to the gruff voice who had been swinging the bag stumbled forward, slightly. She looked down. He'd slipped on an open box of pizza. He'd been awaiting resistance to his swing, and his body hadn't been prepared for open air, and then when his foot landed, it didn't strike carpet but pizza. He stumbled half a step forward, head facing the floor, again, Chrissy assumed, a result of his miscalculation, and what looked to be a large veggie with extra cheese.

Chrissy couldn't help but notice the broad shoulders on her attacker as he stumbled forward, or his strong back as she quickly spun around him and bashed her work bag into his neck. She also found herself impressed that a man this strong and large was not just tough enough to grunt off the impact of a bag containing what police would call "two blunt objects" but that he was nimble enough to keep his wits and dance away from her.

Chrissy was more than a bit worried about this. Who was this? Was he a partner to the man upstairs? She heard another crash from above and assumed he wasn't actually the attacker from upstairs. Her mind raced. He couldn't be the father, or uncle, or even a neighbor who knew Nev well. He had asked if she was Nev when he'd entered. So he couldn't know the girl, at least not well. That made Chrissy happy.

Chrissy even found herself blushing a little, and smiling. This man wasn't attached to Nev, and at least from behind, he thought she might be an 18-year-old beauty queen. He hadn't seen her scars. He'd only seen her from the back. But maybe she still had it.

Nice compliment or no, Chrissy knew she had to get rid of this intruder. In being here, seeing her, even from behind and even if he was impressed, he was no different than the parents she'd left behind at the homes of others of her girls.

"No special treatment for broad shoulders," she thought. "Not even if he gives me a whistle."

The problem, of course, would be getting into her bag and finding her gun. He didn't look the sort of man who would simply wait for her to fish through her purse. He had already tried to knock her out from behind. He really was a man of action. A strong, decisive man, the sort who could ...

She didn't find this line of thought productive. She had a job to do, and he was in the way. It really was no fair distracting her at this time. She'd sneaked her hand into the work bag and was gripping the pistol stock when he raised his head back up and she saw his face and she stopped moving. She stopped breathing. The sounds from upstairs vanished and all she could hear was her heart beating, and as she listened to that beat inside her mind she was convinced she could hear, behind her beating heart, the footfalls of another beating heart, perfectly aligned with hers. She lived in this silence until she was interrupted by that gruff voice.

"You?" it said. "How can it be you?"

Chapter 27

May 18 9:34 p.m.

"How can you be here?"

Yet there she was again. That scarred mouth, turned up in a smile, a slight blush to her cheeks. And that look in her eyes? How could she be both so beautiful, and so ferocious? She was prey and predator, wrapped into a perfect package.

Coach, for the second time today, was overcome with how beautiful the world could be. And just now she'd upped the ante. The way she moved, athletically pure. That had been unexpected.

"People our age don't take training seriously," he was thinking. "She does."

He was glad the bag containing his high school discus and 12-pound shot put had missed. He might yet have to put her down, collateral damage was inevitable. But this moment, he could cherish this fleeting moment for the rest of his life.

In his mind, he was already cataloguing the vision in front of his eyes among his moments of surpassing beauty. If he had to rank them, this was definitely top five. Maybe it was top three.

"What is she looking for in that bag?" he wondered when his mind returned from its happy wandering. Then he asked out loud. "What are you looking for?"

"Why did you take a swing at me with that purse thing," she answered. "And why are you here at all?"

"It's a carrier, a shot and discuss carrier," Coach replied, then he chuckled. "It does kind of look like a purse."

"Odd. So why are you here?"

"I have business here," he said. "I'm completing a project. I need something from the person who lives here. Why are you here?"

He noted that she stopped searching her bag at his answer.

"I'm on a project, a mission of mercy sort of thing," she said. "I'm here to see the girl who lives here. Nev Sparrow."

"That's who I'm here to see."

There was an awkward pause. Coach didn't like this pause. He'd been thinking about what he would say to this woman since he first saw her, and he'd hoped it would go better than this.

"I'm sorry I took a swing at you. I thought you were someone else. I'd never intentionally hurt you."

"But you would hurt Nev? You were planning to hurt Nev? You asked if I was her, then took a huge swing before I could answer."

"Sorry."

"Well?"

"Uhm, as I said, I'm completing a project, and she's part of it. I've only seen her in video, and you look like her from behind."

Chrissy blushed a deeper red.

"That's sweet. From behind, I look like a teen beauty queen?"

"Oh, uhm, I meant Nev, you look like a young soccer player."

"Nev's a beauty queen."

"She was all Colorado three times. Hell of a left leg."

This led to another pause. For a second, they just stared at each other. Then, as they stood in silence, Coach watched her arm retreat from her bag, clutching a pink pistol with an incredibly long pink barrel. Before she could level it at him, he threw his carrier into her work bag. This had the desired effect of knocking her off balance, and he crashed into her, taking her to the floor.

Coach knew enough about wrestling to end this tussle quickly. Before she could react, he was straddling her torso and had pinned her arms above her head. In this position, she couldn't shoot him, at least, he figured. He had to admit, though, that she felt good against him.

"Sorry about this, ma'am," he said. "But I can't let you shoot me. Why did you pull the gun?"

"Why do you think I pulled the gun," she answered. "I was going to shoot you."

"Fair enough, but why did you have a gun in your bag in the first place? Why are you here?"

"I have my reasons. Why are you here."

As he was sitting astride her, he was becoming more and more conscious that, for the first time he could remember, the body contact was leading to an erection. He shifted himself to make that less obvious to her.

"Okay, same answer. Maybe we just got off on the wrong foot..."

He noticed her smile broaden as she interrupted him.

"It's not your foot that's getting off, is it?"

Coach felt himself blush. He was happy to see that she was blushing as well.

"What's your name, can I ask that?"

"Call me Chrissy."

"Call me Coach, or Carl. Or Coach Carl. That's what most people call me."

"Hi Coach." Coach had to admit he liked the look in her eyes. He felt a connection to this woman that he never felt, except perhaps to his donors. He liked the way her muscles moved beneath him. He liked her small, strong frame. He realized, he really liked quite a lot about this woman, and he liked quite a lot about her quite a lot. A thought popped into his head. "Is this what they mean by love at first sight?"

He felt her breath beneath him, and noted that she seemed at ease with this situation.

"Chrissy, I'd like to release you."

"If you have to, then fine."

"But I have to know, if I let go of your arms, are you going to shoot me?"

"I don't know. If I wiggle a big more, are you going to shoot me?"

Coach involuntarily choked. Then he laughed. When Coach laughed, Chrissy laughed.

"This is a moment. We're having a moment," Coach thought, before realizing he was speaking out loud.

"Yes, I think we are. You're strong. I like that, even if it means I can't get free to shoot you. I can see in your eyes, you're not going to hurt me."

Coach thought back through his life. It had been years, a decade or more, since he'd felt anything like this for anyone but a donor. Once he'd found his mission, his mission had become his entire passion in life. No one outside of his freezer group could possibly understand. He could sense that in every conversation he had, with every single mom, with every guy who wanted to bond over a drink, with every fellow teacher or opposing coach. He could always sense that his mission, his artistic vision, left him outside looking in on the rest of humanity.

It was often so with artists.

Yet, here, in this woman, this Chrissy, he couldn't see or feel that sense of disapproval. Coach was searching her eyes for signs of a middle-class morality that would dismiss him as a lunatic, a psychopath, a monster to be feared, and there were none. Instead, he could sense a deep connection.

Coach had hidden himself from the rest of the world because he had always known that there was no option for him but to hide his true self. But was she a soul mate? Coach knew from years of competition that there was no reward without risk, there was no glory for those who refused to chance ruin.

"This is a three-pointer from the center circle," he said. "But I need to know why you're here to see Nev. Are you here to kill her?"

He noted the pause in her eyes. He could sense that there was shock, but not outrage.

"I might… why do you ask?"

"Because I am," he said. "I've never felt this connection before, never with anyone. But I feel it in you, and I feel that I can admit it. I'm here to kill Nev Sparrow. I'd hoped to have done it and be driving away from town to dispose of her body by now."

147

Chrissy wasn't horrified. She was still smiling. In the pause, he could feel her relax underneath him.

"I'm here to save her," she finally answered. "But yes, I suppose, you could say, technically, that I am here to kill her, too."

Coach could feel his soul soar. "I knew it," he said. "I could sense it, I could feel it in you. I could feel the connection in the first second I saw you. We were meant to find each other. Both of us, showing up in this house on this night, in this moment, this is fate."

Coach watched as Chrissy's eyes softened. He could see that she was feeling the same things he was. It was a miracle. It was another of moments of beauty in life that left you convinced that there had to be a God, a God who loved you and directed your life, because nothing this perfect could happen by chance.

"If I could ask," Coach began. "Why are you here, for Nev?"

Chrissy didn't hesitate before answering. It was as if she'd had the answer framed and queued and ready to go forever, and had only been waiting to blurt it out.

"Because she's a beauty queen, at the peak of her beauty," she said. "Nev is the reigning Miss Teen Colorado. She is an ideal, desired by all.

"But I experienced that life. I know it doesn't last. I lived through the horrible pain of beauty fading. I know how every day from this point on in her life will be a step deeper and deeper down into a dark abyss. Her looks will fade, her body will sag and puff up. I lived through this pain, and I have to save others from it, when I can. That's why I'm here, to save Nev."

Coach could barely breath.

"But you're beautiful," he gasped. "You're lovely."

"I'm a shadow of what I was. I'm hideous today. I used to stop traffic. Today I wait at the light, like everyone else. She shouldn't have to live through this. I didn't want that for any of my girls, not in New Jersey of Delaware or Oregon, or anywhere."

148

Coach was stunned. To him, Chrissy was the picture of loveliness. How can she not know?

But he considered her words and he could see her point. It is always, he knew, important to consider life from the perspective of others.

"I'd never agree that you're less than beautiful," he finally answered. "But I see your reasoning. Too many people wouldn't see this, but you're really very kind. You have a beautiful soul to match your physical radiance."

They stared into each other's eyes for a second before Chrissy said, "And you? What's your story? Why are you here?"

"It's nothing as noble as your calling," he said. "I'm almost embarrassed to share my project with you."

"Please do," she said, in a breathy voice. "I want to know."

"It's about creating and preserving athletic perfection. Nev is the last piece of a years long puzzle I've been putting together. I can show you, if you like to see?"

"I think I'd like that," she breathed. "But first?"

"We should kill Nev," he answered. "We can do it together."

"Isn't that a bit intense for a first date?"

Coach blushed.

"I'm just saying, since we're here. If you need to, you can end her life. I just need her left leg."

"Okay, it's a date."

With that, he leaned down. He could feel her breath on his lips just before he kissed her, and just before she kissed him back. His hands left her arms to travel down her body. She wrapped her hands around him, still clutching the pistol. When she pushed on his left shoulder, he rolled over onto his back, and she was now on top of him.

She reached out to the couch to their left, and carefully placed the gun there, then lowered herself for another kiss before rising and peeling off her shirt as his hands slid up her sides.

Chapter 28

May 18th 9:30 p.m.

Nev made herself take a deep breath and think. She was staring at the base of her parents' landline in her dad's office and wondering where the heck the phone part of it was. She had a vague memory of hiding the stupid thing as soon as mom and dad had been out the door. Really, who needs a landline?

Well, right now, I do, she thought. That kind of sucks.

Nev hated irony. She admitted she could enjoy irony in, say, a book or on a TV program if it was handled well. But this? She failed to find the humor in the fact that she had intentionally created this problem for herself. She had acted impetuously, without considering this particular possible situation, and now she was in trouble because of it. Fine, she'd frequently argued with her parents that the landline was a waste of money. It was pointless. It was ancient history.

Their argument had always been something about being old. Oh, and safety, what if the cell phones don't work and we need the police or fire station.

"It pisses me off when they're right," she thought as she opened another drawer to ransack looking for the phone part of the deal.

On the other hand, she wasn't sure this was technically an emergency. True, some psycho idiot was on the floor next to the living room. But she'd kicked his ass once, already. Go me, she thought.

She did a little fake shadow box at the memory of taking the man down so easily, and so completely.

"I am a bit of a badass," she thought. In any case, Bro would be here any minute, and he was a total badass.

Still, find the phone. Her first thought was across the hall. She'd probably put it in her room. Not that there was any reason to hide it there, but she thought "That's where I'd be sure to find it, if that's where I put it.

She went to her desk and chest of drawers and night tables and was opening and closing drawers. She was getting a little antsy. There was a deadline on finding this phone, or rather a crazed killer line. As she was dumping drawers onto the floor the thought occurred to her that she really had a lot of crap stuffed in drawers.

"Why do I have so many Chapsticks? I must have 50. And why do I have lipsticks, as well? I don't wear lipstick. Not often. Sometimes, I guess."

Still, those made more sense than the toy figurines she was finding by the handful.

"Aw, Belle and Ariel," she thought. "Oh, and Sebastian!"

As she dumped the rest of the contents of that drawer, creating quite a bit of noise ("Maybe not really smart, given the circs") she was now singing "Under the sea" to herself, but in an inside voice.

Later, if pressed, she would probably admit that the singing, the dumping of drawers and the daydreaming all played a pretty significant role in explaining why she didn't hear crazy old tweed man coming up the stairs until he was crossing her trophy room, when she heard his labored breath and footfalls as he shuffled and stomped from the stairs toward her.

"Holy crap," she thought as she turned. "He had another knife? How did I miss that?"

Damn, he'd freed his sword. Well, of course he freed the sword.

"Come on, Nev," she yelled at herself, but only inside her head. "You've seen the movies. They always find the lost weapon. Crap."

What surprised her was the knife. It looked exactly like the ones in the kitchen. Damn. It wouldn't have been totally embarrassing to have moved the knives with her into the basement. It would have been smart. Lesson learned, she thought.

Not that they'd help if they were down there. She was a long way from the basement. True, a crazy man wouldn't not now be threatening her with her own stupid knife, but he would have his sword.

"This is not a good situation to be in," she understated to herself.

She was kind of trapped. "Think, Nev. Think."

From the way he moved, Nev knew perfectly well that if she had a bit of space, she could cause this idiot all kinds of trouble. She could run, and he moved pretty slow, for one thing.

But there was no place to run up here so that was a pointless way of thinking about her current predicament. She was going to have to deal with him, again.

"How?"

For the second, she could think. He'd been standing in the doorway, looking back into the small chamber that led into her bedroom, and he was staring.

He turned towards her.

"Ms. Sparrow, you've got an impressive collection of awards," he finally said.

"Thank you," she said, a bit uneasily. "So that's why you're here? To congratulate me then kill me."

The Professor paused, scrunched up his brow.

"Kill you?"

"You already stabbed me."

"Oh, yes, that. I'm afraid that too many of my students refuse to willingly sit for my exams. That was merely an attempt to establish dominance, as a means to compel you to accept that you really must sit for my questioning. It's quite important."

"Sit? So you can stab me again? I don't think so."

The Professor held up the knife and the sword and gave her a slight smile.

"I'm afraid in this argument I possess the stronger position," he said. "I admit, you caught me by surprise. But having now seen your collection of athletic awards, I won't be so easily caught out again. Young lady, I will have you know I'm an excellent molder of young minds. You'd do well to heed me. I have some advice on how your paper on Lincoln failed, and you should listen. I was at Yardton…"

"These other students of yours," she said. "What did you teach them?"

"I taught them as much as I could, in the short time we had together," he said. "Sadly, none of them proved worthy continuing our lessons."

Nev knew she needed a new approach. This was a dangerous idiot she was dealing with. What did she know about him? "Who wears a tweed jacket when they come to kill someone," she wondered. He'd mentioned Yardton, and he said he was here about her Lincoln paper. So, arrogant, annoying? Probably a bit fragile in the ego department. He's quite stabby, so that's something to worry about. But he's not a physical threat outside of that.

Nev's eyes searched her room. "Is there anything here I can use to defend myself?" she wondered. Nothing. Why don't I keep a room full of shields and throwing stars, she thought. Then she noticed the solid oak of her desk chair. She'd pushed it away from the desk. If she could get her hands on that, she'd have a chance. Sadly, it was far enough away that even a quick dash for it would end with getting stabbed at. Her leg hurt. She wanted to avoid that, if possible.

She wondered if she could throw something at him, then while he was recovering, grab the chair and bash him. Then she could dash past him and out of the house, and keep running. She realized she was holding something. She checked her hand.

"Crap," she said as she realized it was Cherry Red, Super Gloss lipstick by Hanoi. "Crap, crap, crap."

Her disappointment was interrupted by his voice.

"These awards, the plaques on the walls and the trophies on the shelves, you won them all?"

"Okay," Nev thought. "He's impressed. I can use that, maybe. How? I guess keep him talking, that works."

"Yeah, yeah I did. I threw away the types they give all kids, participation stuff. These are the ones I won."

"Are they all sporting awards?"

"No, no, not all of them. There are the academic ones, as well."

He raised his eyebrows, as if to speak but instead he took a step back into the trophy nook and was studying them quite intently.

"I see that now, but they do extend beyond the academic," he said. "I find that extremely interesting. I do commend you for being proficient in both the humanities and sciences. Too often, we focus on one at the expense of the other. This appears to be a mistake you have not made. You are to be congratulated."

"Yes, thank you."

"You've also avoided the trap of ignoring physical fitness to focus solely on mental fitness. Mens sana in corpore sano, or as we'd say in this nation ..."

"Sound mind, sound body," Nev cut in. "Yeah, I know that one."

"Intriguing," the Professor said and he smiled, though the way his mouth turned up made Nev think of the Joker's smile, just before things got nasty and Batman had to show up and save the day. "Awards for fitness and academic improvement. Very rare today. I'm afraid."

"And there's one for beauty." Nev said it quickly, hoping to keep him distracted. She was not prepared for his reaction.

"Is there? My word. That is quite interesting."

For the first time his eyes were fully turned away from her. He seemed excited at the prospect that she was a beauty queen. He had no idea it was a bit tarnished. He was clearly impressed.

"Of course he is," she thought. "He may be a crazy man with a sword, but he sees himself as a professor, which means at some level he's a nerd. He keeps spouting Latin like it's impressive. He's showing off. This is his version of flexing in the gym. He's turned on by being around a beauty queen. Jeez. What a dork. I can use that."

Nev realized the item in her hand was a sort of weapon in this setting. She used her thumb to pop off the lid then gripped the base with one hand and twisted the bright red up. She glanced into her bedside

156

mirror as she smoothed the lipstick over her top lip, lightly, then pressed her lips together. That would work, she hoped.

"The statue is actually downstairs right now. The plaque is here, though. Miss Teen Colorado. It's the one with the photo in it."

The professor's eyes were searching the room and then lit up when he found the plaque.

"Oh, oh my, isn't that wonderful. Miss Teen Colorado. The roses, the sash, and they even gave you a crown? So you're the most beautiful young woman in the entire state?" he turned to look at her, his eyes glassy. He saw the bright red shine of her lips and was momentarily taken aback.

"I was wearing this same lipstick when I won the pageant," Nev said, noting she'd nailed it on this one. "I thought you would appreciate seeing it on the pageant winner in person, as well as in the photo."

The professor tried phrasing a response, but it came out as a jumbled mumble.

Wow, Nev thought. This crap actually works. Men actually are pathetic. Once again, thank you television!

"Since you saw the award, I didn't want to disappoint. I know you're a man of letters, a man of the world even, I know you must see beauty queens all the time. I didn't want you to be disappointed, you know" she pursed her lips and thought to herself "OMG I am not actually going to say it" then continued by adding, "by little old me."

She finished by biting her lip. And then, what the hell, she added an eyelash flutter.

In her mind, she was rolling around on the floor laughing. But the words appeared to have had the desired effect. The look in his eyes was priceless. She could practically see his brain turning to goo.

She could hear him swallow, and again. Good, he's flustered.

"You said something about an exam?"

"Test? Yes. Me. Teach. Professor. Test."

"Sounds fascinating," Nev said quickly, and gave him another flutter, just for good measure.

"Mhm mhm," the Professor agreed. "Important. Society, knowledge. Future."

Nev considered whether she should trot out the other standards of comical movie seduction.

"Should I bend over to pick up a pencil," she thought. She couldn't stop the laughter in her head, though, and figured it was best not to push it. He appeared caught by the schoolgirl fantasy. Play to my strengths. Find his weaknesses. She knew this well from soccer, and, in truth, wasn't this sort of seduction a kind of sport? In soccer parlance, she'd just discovered this idiot couldn't turn to his left. In soccer, that meant it was time to attack his left side. In this, she just had to keep the act going.

She gave him her most radiant smile.

"I can see that it is important, knowledge and the future and all," she said, pitching her voice a bit higher than normal. "Man, if this guy wasn't a psycho I would be seriously embarrassed by this," she thought. "But he is."

"Well, if a man as smart as you insists that the test is important, and came all the way out to this little town to give it to me, who am I to say no?"

"Okay," she thought. "He's got to see through that. Give it to me? Jeesh."

Using her peripheral vision only, she took a look at the chair near the desk. It was the third point in a triangle, about equidistant between each of them, and equal to the distance between the two of them, as well.

Bad odds, she thought. "If I can cut the distance to the chair." This guy is a psycho, and he has some very pointy things with him. But he isn't quick enough to deal with me in a fair fight.

158

Nev flipped her hair, smiled and by the time the Professor was done being dazzled by the move she was half a step closer to the chair.

"That's seems more, uhm, than fair," he said, and she could hear him swallowing with each word.

"Okay," she thought. "Final push. Lay it on thick."

"Do you give it to me at a desk or orally?" She emphasized the word oral, not in a slutty way, but a way that made it clear that she was aware of the different meanings of her question. She also moved half a stop closer to the chair.

Actually, thinking about it, there probably was only one way to interpret the way I asked that question, she thought.

"I, uhm, ask the questions, and the student answers. It is, uhm, as you say, not written but spoken."

Well, look at him. Blushing. Shy. Stuttering. She had him.

"This test," she said. "I won't be expected to know as much as you do, will I?"

"Well, uhm, no, course not, but, uhm. But you'd be wise to be, uhm, a bit, ahhh, worried?"

"Because you're so smart. You've had a lifetime of study to shape your mind. Me, I mean, bloop."

In her mind she was screaming with laughter. "Bloop? What the fuck is that? Don't get too cocky Nev. Never stop running before the whistle blows and the game is over."

Still, as she made the odd sound she outlined her figure with her hands, and bounced a little. Nev's hope was that the sway of her breasts would hide the fact that she was now just out of reach of the chair. She would not have believed this could possibly work as a strategy, but she admitted her opinion of adult males was falling with every snippet of conversation with this maniac. Somehow, her over the top deferential bimbo act was working. "Sitcoms speak the truth," she thought.

Still, the crazy man was still holding two very pointy and scary looking blades. To this point, he had lowered them, a sure sign that he was reducing his guard. He hadn't yet let his guard down all the way, however. That's what she wanted, in an ideal world. "Well, in an ideal world, I wouldn't be looking at a murderous dweeb in my bedroom."

Still, lowered blades were better signs than blades at full attention.

"God, now I'm doing the double entendre crap in my internal monologues," she thought.

"So you think I should be worried about the test?"

He swallowed hard, his eyes moving back and forth across the room.

"The others were, worried, or afraid, of the test. I mean my other students."

"Have there been a lot of others?"

"Not so many, but, uhm, yes, I suppose. It depends upon your perspective."

He was now staring at the ceiling, thoughtful.

"Well," Nev said. "I suppose if you say I have to take it, you should give it to me now. Should I take a chair?"

She was now standing next to the heavy oak chair she used at her desk. It had four legs, no wheels. It weighed solid 20 pounds, though. It wasn't a sword, or even a knife. But if she got it moving towards him with enough speed it would be more than a match for either, or both. Mass times velocity and all of that.

She bent over the chair, and heard the gasp he made as he tried not to whimper at the sight of her ass. Her right hand closed around one of the sturdy pieces of the chair backs frame.

"And, bingo," she thought. In her bedside mirror she could see him trying to fumble with the satchel he was wearing, which was impossible as he was holding the blades, so he placed them down and reached inside the bag, taking his eyes away from her.

160

"In his mind, I'm already dead," she thought. "I, however, am not in his mind."

"You see, uhm, I'm afraid my other students have, you know what they say, taught the teacher, heh-heh, that, well, I will have to tie you to the chair. The test can get intense, and my previous students haven't, uhm, done so well."

"Maybe you're just a crappy teacher."

Chapter 29

May 18ᵗʰ 9:32 p.m.

The Professor realized it had probably been unwise to lose his focus, even for a few seconds. That thought was racing through his mind when he heard Nev's voice suggest that "Maybe you're just a crappy teacher." As he glanced up, he couldn't help but notice that the languid, giggly, even sexy school girl he'd been getting along with so well had turned into a flurry of motion. Even as he was pulling the ropes from his satchel with which he thought she'd just agreed he would tie her to the chair, she spun around with the chair in her right arm and in a arc heading directly at his head.

"Clever," he thought. "The sexy school girl actions were part of a ruse, I did underestimate this one."

He couldn't finish that line of thought, however, as the chair crashed into him, sending weapons he'd balanced on the table next to him clattering to the floor, and him stumbling back across the room until the back of his head cracked against a shelf, and trophies spilled down on the top of his head.

Before he had a chance to move, Nev was across the room and confronting him. She gripped his lapels with her hands and when she reared her head backwards he feared she would shake him or spit on him or do something similarly vile.

Instead, the girl sent her forehead flying into his nose. He cracked back again into the shelf, which sent him stumbling back into a second collision with her forehead.

He screamed, and he realized it was a scream that might not be met with respect by the more macho sorts of the world. Still, he was being subjected to pain at a level he could not remember previously, and he did not like it.

He screamed again. He also began crying when he noticed he was now freely bleeding.

Nev wasn't a fighter, but she knew how to head a ball with force, and she knew to use the sweet spot on her forehead. Nail it and it was wicked, no pain for her but could redirect a ball with quite a bit of force. In this case, she was redirecting a head. The physics were basically the same, though.

After that, he was just a woozy old man.

"What the hell is going on?" She wondered about the psycho Bro had been telling her about earlier, the one who went after smart kids. Man, that would be a kick, she thought. Bro tells me about this idiot, races home because he freaks out, and I hand him over.

"It doesn't get much better than this," she thought. Still, if the smart guy went after smart kids, she supposed it wasn't the other moron, the one who went after athletes. That would be a much scarier fight. This guy was 90 percent arrogance.

Still, she would not ignore the warnings of the horror movies. She had no intention of leaving him standing, or conscious.

The beating was now rather routine. He had no fight in him. Still, she needed the phone to call for the police, and it didn't appear she had hidden the phone up here. Why wasn't Brody here? He should be any minute. She had to get this guy downstairs, though. Maybe that was where she'd hid the phone.

She made a plan, beat him towards the stairs. Without his knife, she'd lost all fear. The "professor" as he called himself stumbled to his feet and she kicked out a knee, then shoved him backwards. She caught his falling torso on her leg and dragged him a couple steps before dropping him. She grabbed his feet and spun him around, dragging him across the wood floor, bouncing the back of his head over the floor jam of the trophy room. This seemed to snap him back awake, and on the landing, he was suddenly struggling to his feet.

Nev danced around him as he rose unsteadily, and watched him take a weak step towards the steps.

"He's fleeing," she thought. "Well, he is supposed to be smart."

Before she could act she heard an odd sound that was almost certainly coming from the living room. From the top of the stairs, all she could see was the disheveled mess she'd left downstairs. But the sound was something like a grunt, and creaking floorboards.

"Cool, Bro must have arrived and is collapsed on the couch," she thought. She didn't have the patience to wait on her pathetic attacker to wobble his way down the stairs, so she stepped forward, yelling "Bro" as she tried to skootch around him.

The Professor lunged at Nev and grunted, "Gotcha," but there was no power left in his voice. Nev did what she knew worked with clumsy attempts at contact, she went with it. She controlled his lunge into her, spinning, falling backwards, but taking him with her, and flipping him over her as she rolled onto her back.

Her legs bumped him, and he wasn't nearly steady enough to hold up under a final bump. Nev watched in amazement as he tumbled down the stairs, head over heels, and landed in a heap, propped halfway up against the front door, which his fall had closed.

Nev was past caring about the state of this particular human being. She came racing down after him, smiling as she looked around the stairway wall, expecting her brother.

What she saw was, without a doubt, what she had least expected. Flesh, lots of it, rolling around on her living room rug.

Her immediate thought was of her Mom and Dad, which made her retch a bit. But before she could peel away her eyes, she'd seen more than enough to realize these people clearly were not Mom and Dad. Mom and Dad, for one, didn't undress each other in the living room.

Still, that was a small win. The two middle-aged people - a big beefy guy and a woman who looked something like one of her mom's aerobics instructors - who appeared to be having sex on her living room rug were strangers.

"Oh my God, gross," she yelled. "Who are you and what are you doing here?"

Chapter 30

May 18 9:32 p.m.

After the victim had been pulled from the wreckage, and they'd gotten his mangled but pretty much living body onto the gurney and into the ambulance, Emergency Medical Tech Martin Kingdom doing a quick search of the clothing he'd just cut off the man when he found a wallet in the man's front pocket. "Hey, we know this guy!" he shouted to his partner.

His partner, driving the ambulance as fast as he could towards the Liberty Regional Hospital, shouted back over his shoulder: "So, we know most people we pick up around here. Is he still breathing, or can I slow down?"

"He's very much alive. But this guy wasn't supposed to be local, from the plates. They were California."

"And he's local?"

"Well, rental car, probably. They're all from California these days."

"And?"

"This is Brody Sparrow, remember him? We played against him back in high school. He went to Chances."

"Is he the one with the younger sister?"

"Yep."

"And he's still alive?"

"He's breathing."

"Then we've done our job. Well done, us."

"Yeah, a good day, we saved a life. Tell you what, we get in, I'll figure out where his folks live these days, and call to tell them what's happening."

"It's better if you let the cops know, and let them handle it. That's their job."

The unconscious Brody Sparrow moaned at that.

Chapter 31

May 18th 9:43 p.m.

Chrissy couldn't believe that after 20 years of cursing her solo fate, she'd finally experienced love at first sight. She knew it was supposed to exist. She'd certainly seen enough rom coms where it played a central role. She'd been reading about its existence in romance novels, and sighing, for most of her adult life. But, until this least expected encounter, in this least likely of all places to find love, she had never experienced that magical flash. She had never felt the cliched moment of clarity that comes in a perfect pair of eyes, or the voice or smile of someone who, until that moment, was a stranger, but is now a soul mate.

Chrissy was in love. She hadn't thought that possible when she'd left on this journey. In this man beneath her, she could sense a deep connection. She could sense a connection she hadn't thought possible during these past 20 years.

"Do you feel this connection, uhm, I don't know your name," she rasped.

"Call me Karl, or Coach, and yes, names don't matter, nothing matters but you."

Chrissy looked down on his face and noted the beginnings of tears forming in the corners of his eyes. A real man who could cry? Jackpot. She tugged at his sweatshirt.

"Ooo, you're a strong one, aren't you, Coach," she said as she peeled it up and over his head. He didn't answer, or at least if he did, his answer was muffled by the clothing. So knowing that words were extraneous to the current situation, she instead leaned into him and nibbled and kissed his hairy chest. "I'm Chrissy. Yummy, you're built like a weightlifter."

"Chrissy," he whispered, making it sound like a prayer.

Skinny little girls, she thought, pursued skinny little boys. But women knew this was what they wanted. His hands held her, just under her armpits, his thick strong forearms gripping her body down towards her hips.

"It unclasps in the front," she said, then enjoyed the look of lust in his eyes as his fingers unsnapped her. She pressed herself down onto him, enjoying the feel of her breasts against his chest. Kissing him deeply.

They rolled over, and she was unsnapping his jeans as he was unzipping hers, and they rolled over again, kicking off their pants and sliding down their underwear. This hadn't happened in decades. It's so wonderful, she thought. She moved into him to make sure as much of her was touching as much of him as possible.

Once more they rolled, and now, again, she was straddling him. She rose up and reached between her legs and found him, ready for her, and right now, in this moment, in this slice of time there was nothing else that mattered to her. She could see in his eyes that he was lost in this world of lust and joy and love and passion with her. The world does not exist outside of this moment. She knew that. Everything that mattered was here, with them.

Their bodies, twining so perfectly and she had him in her hand, positioning him perfectly.

"Oh," she gasped as she began to lower herself onto him.

From outside of their bubble she heard an "Ooof." That was followed by thud, thud, crash, fa-thud, and then out of the corner of her eye she could see a man in tweed jacket rolling down from the steps and across the floor and bam, colliding with the door which closed bang.

"What the hell is he doing here," was her first thought.

"Where the hell am I?" was her second.

Beneath her, Coach sat up quickly, almost violently. Chrissy thought the result of that sudden movement was interesting, but was reaching the conclusion that this wasn't the right time.

When did I get an antique looking couch? Where did I find this rug? These thoughts quickly became "Oh my god, I'm not at home. So where am I?

This line of thinking was interrupted, however, by a younger woman's voice.

"Oh my God, gross," Chrissy heard her screech. "Who are you and what are you doing here?"

Chrissy looked up and saw her face as it came down the stairs into the living room. Oh, right. Now I remember.

"Nev Sparrow?" she said.

"Nev Sparrow," Coach exclaimed.

"Oh my god, oh my fucking god, it's like walking in on my parents... what are you doing, who are you, why are you here..."

"You're Nev, aren't you? Sorry, we – the two of us - didn't expect to meet. This is new. This wasn't planned, it's love."

"It is, isn't it. It's magic..."

"What do you think you're doing? This is my house, what are you doing? Get out of here!"

Nev's voice was a bit shrill. Chrissy couldn't help wondering if that hadn't lost her points among, at least, the female judges. While on that thought train, Chrissy noted that Nev was considerably bulkier than most of her girls. Coach had said she was an athlete. Poor girl, she thought, that will all turn to fat in a couple years. I got here just in time, really.

Which is when the situation finally, really sank in. The thoughts came rapid fire.

"I'm naked."

"I'm on top of Coach."

"I'm in love."

"This still isn't the time for, well, this."

"Oh, that's right, I still have to kill Nev."

"No, that was before I met Coach. I'm different now. I've changed. It's not about me. Now it's that we have to kill Nev."

She turned her eyes back to Coach, and could feel the love coming out of them.

"We have to get dressed, you know."

"I know."

"ABOUT DAMN TIME."

"We can pick up where we left off later."

"I'd like that."

"But only after we're done, here."

"I'm calling the police! I swear, just as soon as I… there it is."

Chrissy saw Nev pulling a walk around phone from a cabinet on the far side of the room. She saw her quickly stabbing three times, obviously 9-1-1 and raising the phone to her face.

"Damnit. Damnit."

"It won't work," Coach said from beneath her. "I cut the lines before I came in."

"What?" she heard Nev shout. "What's wrong with you people?"

"Aren't you wonderful?"

"Thanks. Right now I feel that I am."

They heard a groan from the door and saw the man in tweed start to stir and heard him mutter, "What fresh Hell can this be?"

Chrissy locked eyes with Coach.

"Okay, we can do this. Together."

"We have to do it together."

"Ha, fresh, but we can. We can kill her together. We are together. We've found each other, and I don't plan on letting go. But I should deal with her, and you should deal with that guy."

"WHAT? Fuck You," Chrissy heard, then the clatter of a vase flying by them and crashing to the floor.

As she stood up, regretting the loss of contact, Chrissy looked down at Coach. There was a slight hesitation in his voice as he said, "But…"

Slipping into her tee-shirt, she popped her head out of the hole and winked at him.

"Don't worry, this is us now. You can keep her leg."

Chapter 32

May 18 9:57 p.m.

Nev was stepping down from the last stair, unable to stop looking at the naked people who had just announced their intent to kill her (and one wanted her leg?). She couldn't breathe. She couldn't even focus on what was going on. She'd heard their words and now she had too many thoughts, too many questions, to know how to react.

Her mind was racing. It wasn't racing at the level she was used to, while playing soccer or working hard on a problem. She'd thought that was fast thinking. This was a hyperdrive version of that. She

173

could sense the stars blurring into lines around her, like in the movies when a space ship hits the gas.

"Oh my God, there are three murderers in my house? There can't be three murderers in my house? That's crazy. That can't happen."

It simply could not be the case. "Maybe I'm asleep? Maybe this is a really bad dream? Why did I watch so many episodes of Criminal Minds? This can't be happening. This sort of thing doesn't happen, not here, not anywhere."

But as much as she would have liked to plop down on the couch and fall asleep and wake to find it was all make-believe, she knew it was real. Nev knew the danger was real. Are these really killers, in my house, talking about me as their victim?

Nev got mad. Furious mad. She wanted to Hulk out and destroy them and if that destroyed the house and the block and the city, well, collateral damage happens. "Dammit, why are they here? Why me? What the hell do they think they're doing here? Fuck them. Fuck them all. I didn't want this, I didn't want anything but to be left alone. Who do they think they are coming after me?"

But she was looking at the two, and she could hear that idiot in the tweed jacket stirring. There were three of them, even if only two were fully conscious. One of them, the man twisting into the sweat shirt was huge, like he'd already Hulked out. Crap.

She wondered if, just maybe there wasn't a way to get them to change their minds. "If I promised I'd forget about them being here, forget their faces, forget everything and let them go about the rest of their sick lives, and that I'd never tell a soul, maybe they'd leave? What do I have that they want, that I could trade to get them to leave?"

But as soon as she had that thought, she knew it was pointless. What she had was her life, apparently. They wanted that. They meant to kill her, and could feel her soul deflating, preparing for the inevitable.

"Oh God, I'm going to die. I'm fucking going to die. There's nothing I can do to stop them. They're psychotic killers, they can't be reasoned with, they can't be bargained with. They won't just leave.

I'm going to die. I'm not even 19, I haven't even had a chance to try out college, and I'm going to die. It's gonna hurt, a lot. Maybe it will be fast, at least."

The tears were just beginning to well up in her eyes when she realized this line of thought was far less than productive. In fact, it was wrong. She was not dead. She was not dying. She had every intention of living through this night. She had plans of living a lot longer than that.

What was the line from the movie about the Hobbits, "There may be a day when our courage fails, but that day is not this day." That was more like it. She smiled. The beautiful thing about a mind in hyperdrive was that she smiled at about the time her foot met the floor on that final step.

What she needed wasn't fear or depression or a deal, she needed a plan, fast. Okay, the first idiot, he was smart enough, but he wasn't strong or fast, so she'd used that against him. The ogre getting dressed was strong, but she didn't sense there was much that was too smart about him. The woman was gooey and weird and creepy, but she reminded Nev of a cheerleader, and Nev had never met a cheerleader she couldn't outrun and outthink.

So what to do?

First: I need to separate these people. Three on one are bad odds. One on one is better. The woman wants to come after me. I need to make sure she does that far enough away from the ogre so that she doesn't get any help if she gets her hands on me. Okay, easy enough. First choice, out the front door and let them try to catch me. Problem, that's blocked. Tweed is blocking the door, and before I could move him, they could both be on me.

Option 2, through the window? Man, maybe, but that's gonna cut me up bad and what's the advantage of making a break only to bleed to death while they catch up?

Option 3: back upstairs. That could work, it would be quick, at least. But if the back stair is locked up there, I'm trapped. Man, did I unlock that thing? Should have made a checklist.

175

So option 4: Basement. Quick to the staircase, three steps, fast steps, grab the rail and spin and jump and duck below the floor. I've done that a million times. This time it has to count. If they both come after me, great, immediately use the back stairway and come up and then to the kitchen. From there, I can at least grab a knife, and close a door. If I get lucky, I can lock them in, and then I've got time to move ass-fly through here and out the front door. They're old, so they're slow. Let's see them catch once I start running. Ha.

Good. Okay, she's got to come after me.

Just as the woman pulled her top into place, Nev was off at the pace she'd unleash when a ball looked like it was simply too far ahead, and heading out of bounds. One, two, three steps in a flash, grab the pillar as she heard the chair behind her crash, meaning the chase was on. Nev flew down the steps just inches above the carpet, and ducked her head at exactly the right moment to avoid braining herself on the drop ceiling. She hit the basement floor and was dashing into what had just been her cocooning room. Damn, the TV is still on.

She heard the clomp of a set of feet pounding down the steps after her, but it was only one set, and it sounded lighter than the ogre would have been.

Mission accomplished, she'd put space between her and two killers. So this was a one on one meeting.

She raced across the family room, to put the bar between her and her attacker, and to have a door right behind her through which she could run when it came to that.

"Game on," she said, and turned to face killer number 2.

Chapter 33

May 18th 9:54 p.m.

Emt Kingdom knew he should be calling the cops, but, hell, he'd played against the guy and he figured he owed it to an old opponent to break the bad news.

He called 4-1-1 and got the number from information. His parents are probably old enough to have a landline, he figured. Then he had them connect him. But instead of a ring or a busy signal, he got a message, "This line is temporarily out of service."

"Crap," he thought. "Stupid thunderstorms. Gave it my best shot."

He hung up and dialed the number for the Chances Police Department, the after-hours number.

"Chances Police, is this an emergency?"

"This is EMT Kingdom. That accident vic, the one we just picked up on 40? He was a local kid, probably coming home to see the family. Brody Sparrow, you know him?"

"Oh God, yeah, he used to be a cop."

"Really?"

"Big time now, FBI. Sad, is he dead?"

"No, no, alive and kicking. Well, alive. Just calling because I tried calling the house and the phone is out of service."

"Stupid thunderstorms."

"Yeah, anyway…"

"Okay, I'll have a car roll by to tell the parents."

"I'd appreciate that. I was gonna tell them myself. I used to play football against the guy. Is that okay? I mean, it's a long drive back, I guess."

"Hey, if you're up for it, go for it. If you'd rather not, let us handle it, it's easy enough. With the storm and accident cleanup, we won't get there for an hour. But it's good news."

"Pretty crappy deal, bad accident."

"Yeah, but he's alive?"

"Okay, I see your point. Yeah, he was beat up pretty bad, but he should live. If you need it for the report, he's at Liberty. He should be here for a while."

"We'll get right on that."

"Ah, hell, I guess I will drive by myself," Kingdom said, and regretted it immediately.

Chapter 34

May 18ᵗʰ 10:05 p.m.

Chrissy went tearing across the living room. Coach would have pointed out that she was only wearing her panties, but time was an issue, and he kind of liked the view.

As she disappeared down the staircase, he heard a thunk, "crap" followed by an "I'm all right."

It didn't take much calculation for Coach to realize he was on the verge of completing not only a Top 10 or Top 5 day, but the best single day of his life.

"Not even close," he thought. "I finally meet the perfect person, fall in love, she falls for me, and I finish my project? And to top that off, she's a woman with whom I can share everything?"

It was so perfect it all left him a bit woozy, and he realized he was making a dopey sort of smile as he pulled his shoes on.

"Nope, bad idea Coach. Never start dancing until you're in the endzone."

It was one of the first lessons Coach tried to instill in every young charge who came into his life. The phrase might have started with NFL players who began their touchdown celebrations before they'd actually scored a touchdown, and were caught and stopped from scoring because of it. Coach framed it that way to his athletes.

"Don't stop working until the game is won," he'd say. "There's always time to celebrate afterwards."

Of course, he'd offer this lesson just before teaching that "Victory isn't about the final whistle. It begins the second you make a commitment to play the game. From that moment onwards, you can never lose sight of what you want. And you want to win."

Coach had to admit this game was not won. First, he might be in love, but love was like any game, he supposed. If he was going to win at it, he had to focus. Second, the girl Nev Sparrow was still quite alive, and he wasn't going to have an easy time getting her left leg as long as she remained so. And third, this man in the tweed, who was he and why was he here, and why had he obviously been fighting, and losing, to Coach's star athlete?

Chrissy would take care of Nev. If they were a team, he'd just have to trust her to take care of her assigned role. His role had been to deal with the man who was now struggling to stand by pushing himself up the front door.

Coach stood up, searched around for his carrier. He swung it casually as he walked across the room, noting the eyes on the man in tweed were getting extremely wide. Coach could understand the man's fear. He was a little fella. Coach didn't make the mistake of completely discounting him at this point. He'd been in far too many contests where first impressions had clearly lied about an opponent's abilities to underestimate anyone. He recalled wrestling matches when he's sent strong, well drilled boys out against what looked to be scrawny beginners. He learned pretty quickly that sometimes the scrawny one was simply wiry. He'd had more than one wrestler lose to opponents who anyone would have declared to be inferior.

The old saying, it's not the size of the dog in the fight, but the fight in the dog, that was a good lesson to carry through life everyday. Coach tried to.

Even so, the man in the tweed, well, he looked beat. To be honest, he looked half-dead. The easy path here would be to take a couple quick steps towards him and take care of the other half of him. One quick swipe of the carrier ought to do it. A 16 pound blunt instrument can do a bit of damage.

Beyond, Coach reasoned, when you have the element of surprise, use it. And, well, quick had its advantages. It would get him downstairs to check on Chrissy faster, for one.

But easy wasn't always best. It would be worthwhile to know who this man was, why he was here. It would be worthwhile to know why Nev appeared to have tossed him down the steps. Coach also wanted to know how she'd done that. He wasn't a big man, but he was an adult man. If Nev was a judo or a karate champion, it would be worth knowing that before he approached her.

So Coach stopped about three feet from the man, looking down on him as he continued to struggle to his feet.

"Hold on there, guy," he finally said. "Before you spend all of your energy standing up, why don't we chat a bit. I don't want you to exhaust yourself only to have me knock you back over. No reason to waste what little strength you've got left."

"Whuh?"

"Hmmm, that bad. Be right back. You got your bell rung, looks like."

Coach walked away and returned with two glasses of water. He splashed one into the professor's face, and handed the other glass to him.

"This ought to bring you around. Drink up."

After the Professor had finished drinking, he handed the glass back with a "Thank you."

"Good, the cobwebs should be cleared now. I've got a couple questions. Care to answer?"

"Do I have a choice?"

"Not really, not much of a choice, I guess. You either answer or I'm afraid I bash in your skull."

"A fronte praecipitium a tergo lupi," the Professor answered.

"What's that now?"

"Ah, of course, no Latin. A precipice in front, wolves behind," he explained. "A precipice is a cliff. You might know the saying better as between a rock and hard place."

"Huh. That's just about right, isn't it. Nice one, wolf and a cliff, you say. I'll have to remember that one. Is that yours?"

"Cicero, I believe."

"The English fella who wrote all the plays? Never been much of a reader, but he seems like a smart one. Caught between wolves and cliff. Ha. Nice."

The professor didn't sense this was the sort of moment that lent itself to correcting his large and scary new confidant. So he fought back the urge to blurt out, "Shakespeare is the smart English fella, Cicero was Roman."

Instead, he steadied himself on wobbly legs, and stayed silent.

Coach paused, and looked him up and down.

"You seem like a smart man, too. What do you choose, the wolves or the cliff?"

"Are you telling me I must choose? Is it one or the other?"

"I'm not a smart one, not like you at least, but I can't see much way around that, can you?"

"I suppose not. The young lady, Nev Sparrow, am I to understand she is your daughter, or perhaps a niece?"

"The answer to that is a big no. No relation."

"Then you are a friendly neighbor, perhaps?"

"Nope, never met her."

"I'm at a loss to see why you have put yourself in the role of her protector in that case."

Coach laughed, a deep throated laugh that the Professor found just as intimidating as his thick forearms and neck.

"That's probably not a good description of my role here. I only know her by reputation. But I was gonna ask the same questions of you. Why are you here, and why did she just throw you down the stairs? You some kind of a pervert?"

"So are you also here because of her psychological profile of Lincoln?"

"Her what?"

"Her psychological profile of Abraham Lincoln, our 13th President. The paper for which she was awarded a Presidential honor. As I'm sure you know, it has many flaws. Is that why you're here?"

"Uhm, no. What are you on about? I don't know a thing about her paper, or her award, and I have no idea if it has flaws."

"You can trust me on this, it is deeply flawed."

Coach adjusted his feet and stared hard at The Professor.

"I don't see why I would trust you on anything right now. But that's not why I'm here. Have to be some kind of crazy to show up at a young girl's house because of a high school paper."

Now it was The Professor's turn to shuffle his feet. He even blushed a little.

"Oh."

"Oops. Sorry. Is that why you're here, this paper?"

"I'm not crazy. It's just that I have a responsibility to ensure that the brightest minds of the coming generations burn truly bright. I was here to see if Ms. Sparrow's mind worthwhile. I wanted to know if, despite this effort, she was worth saving."

"Well, takes all types."

"Why then are you here? You introduce yourself as a fellow stranger in his house?"

"Oh, me, that's simple. Nev's a hell of a soccer player. She's got a wicked left leg."

"And you're one of these athletic scouts?"

"No, I'm, well, I guess I can tell you, seeing as I have this," Coach said, raising up his carrier, a move which also showed off a right arm that bulged in a threatening fashion. "And seeing as you aren't likely to make it out of here, I'm here for the leg."

"Oh, my."

"Gotta say, a decade of silence, and now I've said it out loud twice in one night and it feels good."

The Professor was silent, looking hard at Coach, to the point that Coach was feeling uneasy. But after a brief pause, his eyes seemed to relax.

"So you're here to kill Nev Sparrow?"

"Technically, I'm here for her left leg, but I suppose it works out to the same thing."

"The odds have to be astronomical," the Professor muttered.

Coach gave him a quizzical look, complete with tilted head and furrowed brow. The intent was obvious, he didn't follow the reasoning on The Professor's comment.

"… just astronomical. You see, I'm also here with, well, less than the kindest motives regarding Ms. Sparrow."

"Meaning?"

"I certainly intended to test her, and I do believe the test is both fair and essential knowledge. But those who fail do tend to die."

"You've killed before?"

"I've failed my share of students, and there are consequences for failure, yes."

Coach laughed again, and this time added a slap on the back for The Professor, which caused the smaller man to stumble forward.

"And you were here to kill Nev tonight?"

"To test her. But if she'd failed, yes."

"Do many pass this test?"

"None so far."

Coach was smiling broadly.

"Boy howdy, three of us at once? This girl is having a very bad night."

It was again The Professor's turn to be shocked.

"Three? But there are only two of us, surely."

"Nev is downstairs. My new friend, number 3 in our accounting, is taking care of her."

"Your friend?"

"Chrissy, she's a peach. She's here to save Nev from growing old and getting ugly. She's really a very kind person. One of a kind. We're in love."

185

"Yet you allowed her to go downstairs in pursuit of this violent young woman? Shouldn't you be down there to protect her?"

"I should be, and I will go soon. First, I'm supposed to take care of you. That was our division of labor. I'm afraid it doesn't look good for you, little man."

"But now that you've gotten to know me and realized our shared mission you're reconsidering?"

Coach paused, and rubbed his chin. He considered the odds against all three of them arriving at the same place at the same time, and wondered if it wasn't a sort of sign that they were destined to work together. They did share a mission, and this little man was obviously a smart one. On the other hand, he'd already had his shot at Nev and had clearly failed.

"You didn't answer my question, wolf or cliff?"

The Professor swallowed hard. This appeared to be the sort of test he would give to a pupil, and such questions rarely ended well for the pupils. But the large man didn't appear to be angry, and hadn't yet injured him in any way.

"I am afraid I am a precipice type," he said. "I suppose I would hope to be able to catch a ledge on my way over the edge. I believe that would be my choice. I've never been the sort to face the teeth and claws."

"Huh, okay," Coach said. Moving quickly for such a large man, he raised his carrier and smacked The Professor hard enough to send him tumbling back onto the ground. There was a satisfying crack of a bone breaking as the 12-pound-shot put crunched into the small man's left shoulder. The immediate result was a sharp scream of pain.

"I'm more of the wolf type," Coach said as he stepped towards his victim. "I'd like my chances."

The Professor stared up at him from the floor, obviously with questions in his eyes. His eyes were darting back and forth, searching for a possible escape route.

186

"But we share the same goal?" he said, through teeth clamped with pain.

"Oh, yeah, as for you joining us, I'm afraid the saying makes sense, two is a company, three's a crowd. It's time I got going."

Coach raised the carrier again, preparing to deliver a final blow. He stopped, however, when he heard another scream, this time from the basement. It also sounded like pain.

"That was my Chrissy," he shouted, and raced toward the stairs.

Chapter 35

May 18th 10:06 p.m.

Nev was in her element when she was on the move. That's always when she'd felt most comfortable, most confident. And right now, she was moving fast. She flew into the family room from the stairs, slamming the door behind her. Then she dashed across the room in five quick steps, vaulting over the bar on the far end and turning as she landed to look back at the doorway from the front stairs.

The door opened slowly. Then the woman's head poked around, cautiously, until her eyes found Nev. She stopped, putting her hands before her, patting down the air in what Nev supposed was intended as a calming manner.

188

"Nev. I'm Chrissy Kristens. I came to see you all the way from New Jersey. See, I used to be a beauty queen, just like you. I understand what you're going through now, and what will come later. I'm so glad we have this chance to chat."

She paused to unzip the black bag she was holding, and pulled out a statue that looked a bit like an Oscar, though a bit more beat up that Nev imagined Oscars to be.

"See, I have a trophy as well," she continued, and nodded at the Miss Teen Colorado trophy next to Nev on the bar.

Nev glared at her, but stayed silent.

"Oh Nev? I'm so sorry it has to be like this."

"It doesn't. You don't have to be here. You can leave."

"But it does have to happen, and I do have to be here. This is my mission. You're too young to know how cruel the world can be."

"So you're going to kill me?"

"I'm going to protect you from all the suffering I had to live through. I know this seems harsh, but the others went happy, and beautiful. That's how it will be for you, still young, still beautiful. Just like when you won your crown."

"But dead."

"Well, yes."

"OMG you're a psycho."

"That's just hurtful. I'm just a woman with a mission of kindness."

"You were just saying you were going to cut off my leg."

"That's just Coach Karl. He's got a different mission. He's a sweet man, but he has his own needs. You won't feel a thing. I swear I will make sure of that. You're one of my girls. I protect my girls."

This caught Nev off guard. Clearly, the crazy lady was telling her that there were other girls who had received this kindness. Her mind flashed back to her chat with Bro. He said one of the psychos killed beauty queens. Which reminded her of the second one he was pursuing, the guy who killed smart kids. Was that the guy upstairs in the tweed? That would make sense.

Holy hell, does that mean the third one, this Coach Karl, was the third psycho killer? The one who killed promising athletes?

Nev could feel the rage swelling insider of her. Stupid fate. This morning Bro is going on about the three killers he's tracking, and this evening they all show up at her house? Except for Bro. He wasn't here. Where the hell is he?

Focus, Nev. This is not the time to zone out. As she paused, the crazy woman started to take a step forward. Bad, Nev thought. Very bad. Keep the distance.

"Nev, it's okay," Chrissy said as she slowly took a step. Nev noticed that as she was stepping the woman caught a glimpse of herself in the small mirror above the piano and stopped to adjust her hair.

"Of course," Nev thought. "She's that type. Makes sense. Maybe I can use that."

"So beauty queens, that's your thing, your mission?"

"Yes, Nev. Really, I'm here, we're both here, because we love you and want the best for you."

"You're so beautiful, surely you were a beauty queen?"

Chrissy stopped, and again looked for the reflection in the mirror. She was smiling.

"I was, a long time ago, that was back when, well thank you, you're very sweet. But when I was your age I really was beautiful, like you are now. That's why I'm here. You don't understand the pain of losing all this."

"What?"

"Losing your looks. Losing your confidence. Losing the ability to make men stammer and other women seethe. Losing the attention that comes with what God gave you. It's horrible. It's torture."

"Worse than death?"

"So much worse. See, death, at least this death, is quick. It's kind. The pain I'm saving you from, that lasts for years, for decades. Other people can't understand, regular looking women who never had the adoration we can expect…"

"I don't expect adoration. I entered the beauty pageant because my Mom wanted me to. I thought it was fun, but kind of pointless."

This froze Chrissy. Nev could tell that she was trying to puzzle out this statement. Clearly, in her warped worldview, women wanted what she wanted, thought like she thought. "I don't think she actually knows many women," Nev thought. "I don't think she knows many people, period."

"But when your beauty fades, you're left alone," Chrissy was blurting out. "You're left to live without love…"

Keep her thinking, Nev thought. She's not moving while she's thinking, and Bro has to be getting near by now.

"You seemed to be doing well with the guy upstairs, with, uhm, Coach Karl, right?"

Chrissy seemed to melt a little, a dopey smile spread on her face. Somehow, she keeps that crazy look in her eyes, though, Nev noted. "The advantage of being truly batshit psycho, I guess."

When Chrissy spoke again, it was almost as if she was forming her words in sighs. "Yes," she finally said, dragging out the "s" in an almost Gollum-in-love fashion. "Tonight is a miracle. It's the most wonderful night. I've dreamt of this forever. I've been alone for 20 years, just me and my girls and my memories, and now, this wonderful man."

Chrissy prattled on about her first glance at Coach, how she'd seen something in his eyes that she knew immediately connected with her innermost self. Right now she was talking about a cheeseburger for some reason.

Nev used the time of this reverie to consider her plan. She's a killer, so that's her advantage. I'm fast, and I'm pretty sure with her, one on one, I'm okay.

"Oh man, oh man, oh man, I can't believe I'm thinking like this," she thought. "And what's in that bag? She had a gun, a pink gun, but if she was going to shoot me, I'd be shot. So pretty sure that's still upstairs on the couch. Crap, I should be sitting down on the couch across from me watching Criminal Minds, not wondering how to outsmart one to avoid getting murdered in the basement. Of course, if I avoid getting murdered in the basement, I've got to figure out how to avoid getting murdered upstairs, for a second time tonight."

She then screamed a little, inside her head. Calm down, calm down. Think.

Chrissy here is obsessed with mirrors, so I should get her into the mirror room. That will obviously distract her. And then, what…

Her eyes landed on the Miss Colorado Trophy. That'll hurt, she thought.

"Okay, we've got a plan. Time to see if it works."

She casually cracked the door behind her open then beneath the bar circled a hand around the trophy.

"When I run, I've gotta make it count," she thought. "No mistakes. Don't underestimate her. She kills people."

"So it really is a miracle, and I think we're going to be together after tonight."

Chrissy was finished. Nev knew what she had to do, but was nervous about kicking off a sequence of events that revolved around her murder.

"So you found love?"

"Yes, I just said so. Are you listening? You really should. I've learned a lot in my life."

"But you just fell in love. Why do you still need to come after me?"

"I don't follow your reasoning. I've told you. I'm here to help, really. I know, now it seems like the world is wonderful and your life will be filled with admirers and beauty, but that doesn't last. It seems like it will, but it won't. You're young and perfect and you can't understand why this has to happen. But it really does. It's you I'm thinking of. A little bit of pain now, but it will save you from so much pain later on."

"But you just admitted that line of thinking is wrong."

"What? How so?"

"You said life is long and lonely and sad, but now you're older and in love, and you're obviously very happy about that."

"I am. It's been a long time, but I am happy right now."

"So what are you really saving me from? Happiness? The chance at love, like what you found?"

"No, I told you, I'm saving you from … oh, my. I see your point. If I can find happiness later in life, why wouldn't you?"

"Exactly. You've shown me love and joy can exist after all this fades," as Nev spoke, she used her free hand to make a circle around herself. Maybe the reasoning can work, she thought. Chrissy looks stumped. Her shoulders look less tense, less ready to pounce.

Nev thought maybe this was a chance. She continued with her logical breakdown of the situation. Logical breakdowns probably have a pretty low success rate with psychotic killers, she thought, so she didn't move her hand away from the trophy, and angled her feet towards the doorway. Keep talking, but be ready to run, and ready to fight.

"You said it yourself, your goal in life is to protect your girls. You said you don't want to harm them, you want to save them. But now, see, it's different. You know that what you're saving us from might also be the wonderful parts of life, falling in love like you have, tonight. Miracles happen, don't they?"

Chrissy looked confused. "You're a smart one, in addition to being a pretty one. Aren't you? I gotta think about this."

After that, she was silent, for a full minute, staring at the floor. Twice, she pulled her head up to talk, but both times she decided on continued silence and lowered her eyes again.

Finally, Nev interrupted.

"It's true, isn't it? You don't have to kill me anymore? You're seeing that you don't need to kill to protect, because you're not really protecting me. You'd just be killing."

"I hear what you're saying," Chrissy finally said. "And I see your reasoning, and it makes sense, it really does."

"So, we're okay?" Nev didn't really have much faith in this, but what the hell, she figured it couldn't hurt to address the crazy lady as a friend. She knew that this really didn't help with the Coach upstairs who, apparently, wanted her left leg, and it wouldn't make a smidge of difference to the professor character who, well, she wasn't exactly sure what he wanted, but it wasn't good. Still, take what you can get, she thought.

She was after all, one of Chrissy's "girls."

Chrissy appeared to, once again, be struggling. Nev knew she was making at least a little progress, at the very least she was buying herself some time, and time worked in her favor. Bro would arrive any minute.

"I didn't leave home expecting to arrive here and fall in love," Chrissy said when she finally spoke. "I expected to arrive and find you, and to help you avoid what was a very difficult time for me. See?"

"Of course, but now you know there's a silver lining to this difficult time. We go through the pain, and I can't imagine, but it must be horrible. I'm impressed by how well you survived it and all. But then, well, you found love. You found happiness. It's inspiring, really."

"Right, yes, I suppose. I don't have to kill you now. I suppose I know that there are better times ahead, that will mix with the worse times ahead, and that it will all balance out and probably tip towards the wonderful because, well, falling in love is something you can't imagine until it really happens."

"So, I should just leave, I think, and give you time to get back to your man … "

"No, see, sorry. I don't have to kill you, I see that know. But I still really want to. I still really feel the need to kill you, tonight, right now."

"Oh."

"See, I've been looking forward to it. It's kind of a shock to realize that. I think maybe the saving my girls line was kind of an excuse my mind had come up with. I think all along, maybe it was about the killing. I really like ending a life."

Nev's eyes were wide open, she was keeping her breathing even and level. But she understood that right now, she was just waiting on the whistle to blow. Once that happened, things were going to get crazy.

"Creepy."

"Yeah, I can see how you'd think that. It is, in a way, but it's really fun in other ways. I like everything about it. I like the violence, the attack. I like watching the life drain from your eyes. I like the ritual. I like the planning. Really, I like everything about it. I love everything about it."

195

Nev understood that this was very bad news for her. Okay, everything is now on being able to take care of myself until Bro arrives.

"Thanks, really, for helping me see the truth. I think maybe I owe this to Coach Karl, as well. I can be who I really am with him, and he accepts me and loves me for it. And who I really am is a woman who just really likes killing girls like you. That's where I find joy.

"So, you know, sorry, but thanks. It's really meant a lot to me."

Nev couldn't find much solace in that. The words "total lunatic" were front and center in her mind. But at least she knew where she stood. At least for another second or two.

With that, Chrissy let out a blood curdling scream and lunged forward. Nev had already grabbed her trophy and was through the door at a full run long before Chrissy reached her.

Chapter 36

May 18th 10:08 p.m.

"The little witch is fast," Chrissy thought as she threw herself at the first door Nev had escaped into. But running away wouldn't save her, no matter how fast the girl ran.

"I've got all night," Chrissy thought. Chrissy knew she would catch Nev, eventually. She always eventually got her prey.

"Never been after anyone so fast," she noted. "But it's nice to be hunting."

There was a certain clarity of purpose in Chrissy's mind right now, and that clarity made the chase thrilling. For a decade, she had insisted that her life had been dedicated to saving young women from the pain she had experienced.

That was true, Chrissy knew that was true. The pain she had experienced had been real, and that pain had been devastating. No one should have to suffer the way she had. She truly did not want girls like her to have to experience the pain of growing old and ugly and soft.

That is, in a sense, a pain worse than death.

But tonight, so many things made sense that she'd never really been able to admit before. She really did not want her girls to suffer. That was true. It also wasn't really true, or at least not the complete truth. Chrissy had to admit that the suffering angle had been a kind of excuse she'd come up with to justify bashing in the backs of her girls' skulls.

Chrissy also had to admit she really liked bashing in a skull.

She loved seeing the blood spray out and later seep out of the wounds she inflicted. She loved standing over her girls, in a position of power, of dominance, and watching the fear in their eyes melt into acceptance that they were weakening and would soon leave. She loved the solid feel of her trophy in her hand, and the sensation of contact. She loved the complete and total release that came with the attack. That release, that freedom to be herself and totally, honestly, herself, had been unmatched in this world, until tonight.

Somehow, against all odds, against what appeared to have been her fate and the flow of the universe, she had found destiny, or it had found her. Coach, or Karl, was it.

Coach. She almost sighed it. Every time she pictured his face, she couldn't help smiling. She wanted to laugh, or to giggle. She wanted to sing.

She had not come to this house, to this job, looking for love. She had come looking for another death. But she could not deny that she had found love. She had known it the first time their eyes met. She could feel it in that second, feel the connection in her heart and stomach and mind.

As she raced across the room she could hear the thumping of Coach's heavy feet on the stairs behind her. How sweet, he's coming to me.

"I could wait for him," she thought.

But she was hunting, and he was hunting. And, well, he'd just had his kill, so it was only fair that she got to Nev first. She would certainly share, afterwards. There was no doubt about that. He said he was collecting body parts, and he could have everything he wanted. She would even help him with that.

But the first blow, she thought as she flew through the door behind the bar to see a second room, that was hers.

She stopped, looked around. This room was odd. Five walls, each with a door in the middle. The light was not only on but almost harshly bright. And there was nothing in the room, except for mirrors. There were dozens of mirrors. Long ones on each of the five doors. Round ones on one wall. Oval ones on another wall. Rectangular mirrors covered two more walls. And the wall just behind her as she came into the room was covered by mirrored tiles.

Chrissy paused, her hand naturally went to her hair. "I should run a comb through it, really," she thought. "Why don't I have a room like this."

Everything in this room was in place, nothing amiss. But while there was clearly no Nev here, the door directly across from her was cracked open, as if it hadn't quite latched while being closed a bit too carefully.

Chrissy dashed across the room. She liked the way she looked while moving. She looked sexy. She liked the way her hips moved. She liked the way her hair moved. She wondered if there was some way to move like this, accidentally of course, for Coach? He'd like this.

She decided she looked as if she was a strong woman with a purpose. Well, she was a strong woman with a purpose. But it was nice to look like one.

"Huh," she thought. "A week ago, I wouldn't have seen the beauty I still have. I only would have seen what used to be in these mirrors, and I would have been crushed. Being in love changes things, doesn't it?"

With her free hand she was reaching out for the door handle. Chrissy was excited.

"Nev, you can't run forever," she yelled when she couldn't resist leaning over for a last peak in the long mirror.

The door exploded into her before she had a chance to react. The corner of the door caught her left shoulder squarely and forcefully, spinning her into the mirror.

The mirror shattered as it smashed into her face, dabbling her face and arms with small cuts. She stumbled back half a step, unable to catch her balance, and more than a little woozy. She tried to blink her way back to consciousness, but Nev burst through the door. The young athlete's legs were spread apart for perfect balance. Her right arm brought her Miss Teen Colorado trophy arcing over her head and down onto Chrissy's neck forcefully and quickly. The snap was loud, and Nev knew even before the scream of pain left Chrissy's lips that she'd broken something, probably a clavicle.

Chrissy crumpled to the floor, dropping with that rag-doll drop of someone who's gone head to the wrong head in a challenge. There were footsteps storming across the basement. As Chrissy's vision faded to black, the last thing she saw was Nev hurtling back through the same door from which she'd launched her counter attack.

She was impressed that her last thought, however, was how Coach would now have to catch and kill Nev, and not what she felt was the more selfish notion if Coach would still find her attractive with all the additional cuts.

"I guess it's a sign that I really do see myself as part of a whole," she thought, before blanking out.

Chapter 37

May 18th 10:13p.m.

As soon as he'd heard the yell, Coach knew that nothing else mattered other than getting to his Chrissy as quickly as possible.

"Stupid, stupid, stupid," he shouted at himself. "Never abandon your partner. Oh god, I'll never forgive myself."

As he bounded down the stairs the thought occurred to him that the scream might have been one of pain or even fear. It might have been one of anger. Did Chrissy scream in anger like that?

He was just thinking "we have so much to learn about each other" when his forehead slammed into the drop of the basement ceiling. The contact, combined with his speed, lifted his feet off the steps, while the momentum of the lower part of his body continued to stream forward. His right arm, gripping tightly to the carrier, seemed to float in front of him, before bouncing off the underside of the ceiling.

His speed then carried his toes into the underside of the drop ceiling, cracking a tile. But at that point, gravity kicked in. Coach fell back to Earth stretched out flat, his back towards the floor. His neck landed first, cracking hard into the last step. His body slammed down a split second later. A split second after that, his heavy carrier smacked back into his face, bloodying his nose.

A lesser man might well have died from that contact. The carrier was no more than a solid punch to the face. That he'd always survive. Coach realized the neck was always one of the more vulnerable points in impact. But his thickly muscled neck was able to absorb the blow well enough. That's not to say he wasn't in pain. It hurt like hell.

His mind flashed back to his college days, playing football, taking a pitch on a reverse and breaking out of the backfield seeing nothing but daylight. At the time all he'd been thinking about was scoring. This was an easy touchdown. He hadn't seen the powerful arm that came from his blindspot on the right. It wrapped around his neck. He'd experienced this exact sequence of events before. Close-lined was the term, he remembered.

He wasn't sure if that memory had come in a daydream or a blackout moment. The two were pretty similar in his experience. Maybe it was a blackout, there were stars twinkling in front of his eyes. He had to admit that if you removed the context, they were beautiful against the white backdrop of the ceiling.

"I've been close-lined again," he thought as he lay on the ground, making sure his fingers and toes were still functioning. "Stupid house close-lined me."

He seemed okay, if bruised. He ran his hand over the back of his head, no blood, no obvious breaks. He breathed deep and stretched his legs and arms.

His hearing was returning to normal.

"The world is always so loud when I come out of a blackout," he remarked. He rolled onto his side and was pushing himself to his knees when he heard glass shatter, wood crack and Chrissy scream again.

He'd forgotten the reason behind his hurry, but it came flooding back.

"That one sounds like distress," he thought.

"I'm coming," he managed to croak. "Chrissy, I'm coming to you."

He shoved himself from his knees to his feet, and wobbled through the staircase door into what looked like a television room, a family room. He could see a bright light coming through a crack in a door on the far end, and heard a whimper from beyond it. He stumbled heavily across the room, throwing up the door just in time to see a door on the far side of the room slam shut, sending a sprinkle of glass shards down onto the unmoving figure of his new love.

He screamed. In that moment, he forgot about Nev, and his project, and even the pain that was hobbling his body. He raced across the room and threw himself to his knees, next to her. Coach couldn't help but notice that there was an echo of Picasso's reclining nude to her position. Her head was bent back awkwardly. Her arms bent behind her at unnatural angles.

"Oh God, she's dead," he thought. "She's so beautiful, and yet she's dead."

He realized however that she was breathing.

"Not dead, knocked out. Still, she's so beautiful."

He noted the sound of footsteps, first heading up stairs, now on the first floor, and realized Nev would soon be out of the house and running for help.

That didn't matter, not now. He needed to capture this moment forever, seal it into a part of his mind that he could reach whenever he needed a reminder that hope does spring eternal. She was alive. Tears trickled down his cheeks as his powerful, stubby fingers started picking shards of glass off her body. It was a gentle action, but he was swift.

He ignored the small cuts digging into his fingertips, and methodically removed every piece of glass he could see. Nothing had imbedded too deeply into her, but she had dozens of tiny, shallow cuts. Threads of red twined across her face and forearms.

"Good girl, Chrissy," he said softly. "You got your arms up in time to take most of the blow. Well done, my love."

He ran his hands over her arms and back and breathed relief at again finding no obvious, serious damage. As he did this, his powerful arms carefully cradled her, and the tears from his face fell onto hers and washed the small circles clean of blood.

"You're going to be fine," he said, holding her and looking closely at her. He bent forward and gently kissed each eyebrow, the tip of her nose and carefully her lips.

As his lips left hers, her eyes fluttered open and she sighed.

"Karl, you came for me."

"Always," he said.

"What happened?"

"I shouldn't have left you alone," he explained. "It looks like Nev was ready for you. She's an athlete. She counter-attacked. I should never have left you to go after her alone. She's different than most of your girls. She's more mine to handle. I'm so sorry. She got away, upstairs. I had to come to you. She's gone now, probably out the front door and running for the police."

"You have to get her. You have to. We need her. You need her. I need her."

"I only need you now," he answered. "I knew that the second I heard your scream. I need you and ... oh wait."

"What?"

"She's still in the house. I just heard footsteps going up steps. It sounds like to the second floor, or the third."

"She's trying to hide? Poor little girl. She has to know we're going to find her.

"No, Chrissy. "I told you, she's not hiding. She's an athlete. She's planning on a fight. This is my game now. You rest for a second and come upstairs when you're ready."

"Oh, Coach, but, I mean can you, is it possible ..."

"Can I leave her alive, alive for you to finish? Is that what you want to say, to ask?"

"Yes."

"Of course, my love."

"Be careful, remember she's strong, and she's violent. She took out me and the man in the jacket."

"Don't worry, we're on my turf now. She's tough, but she's about to learn a lesson in brutality."

Chapter 38

May 18ᵗʰ 10:21 p.m.

Emergency Medical Tech Martin Kingdom wasn't at all sure it had been a good idea to make the drive. Sure, he'd played football against the guy, Brody Sparrow. And sure, the guy's kid sister was cute. But he'd never delivered bad news, and now, standing on their front stoop, he wasn't at all sure this was a good idea.

First of all, he'd romanticized the house on the way over. The family, he'd convinced himself would be one of those totally together households, everything in order. Instead there was a pizza box on the front stoop and while that didn't say much in and of itself, it wasn't a good sign.

Beyond that, while actually standing on the front porch and realistically imagining the conversation he was about to have, well it didn't sound as cheerful now as it had on the drive over.

"Hello, I'm here to tell you your son is alive," didn't sound nearly as upbeat as it did among emergency workers. And he really wasn't at all sure that explaining how everyone working the case had been sure Brody would die before he reached the hospital would offer the tale much of a pick me up.

"That's the problem," he thought. "Most people don't deal with the stuff we do, and will go their whole life without having to see what we see all the time."

Which left him more than a little terrified at what he had to do. The easy out would be to sneak back to his car and drive home, letting the Chances Police Department know he hadn't been able to make it over after all.

"Am I that much of a chicken?" he wondered, and answered "No, but just about."

He also, however, wasn't able to stir up the courage to knock or ring the bell.

The compromise between fleeing and knocking was standing here, which he realized also was not much of a long term strategy. Instead, using the stoop rail as support, he leaned over so that he could peak in the main window.

What he saw far exceeded a pizza box on the stoop. The room was a mess, broken tables and chairs. There were even a couple pieces of underwear visible. He leaned a bit more and saw the shoulder of a man in a tweed coat slumped over, trying to pull himself towards the stairs. On the couch, there was even a pink handgun. And just as he was thinking, "What the hell" the guy's sister came into view. Nev was her name. She was running for all she was worth through the living room, holding a white bucket with a blue lid and handle.

He saw her rear back and swing her leg at the figure in tweed. While he couldn't see any contact he was pretty sure he heard some. After that, she was racing up the stairs.

EMT Kingdom stepped back into the center of the stoop to think about all this. None of this made any sense. Was it some kind of family game night gone crazy? Had they heard about Brody's accident and lost their minds?

He was standing there, puzzling over the situation, when he heard what he was pretty sure was Nev's voice shouting. "Come and get me, you psycho asshole!"

It was a rather emphatic yell. She sounded really angry. So, the guy in tweed is a psycho? That would explain why she kicked him, I guess.

He leaned back towards the window to take another peak and was just in time to see a very large, strong looking man rumble into the main room from around a corner (stairs?). The man was a bit wobbly, but still looked menacing. He was carrying what looked like one of those track and field bags for holding a shot put and a discus.

"Okay, it can't be that," he reasoned. The large man looked down at the floor and said "You're still around, and swung his bag at him. Again, Kingdom could hear the contact.

After that, the large man was soon climbing the steps, following Nev.

"Holy shit," Kingdom thought. "He's the psycho, and he's after her. Maybe the guy in tweed is her father? No, that makes no sense. She kicked him. Maybe it's the guy's partner?"

Does it matter, he wondered. He had two choices, and he had to chose now. Either open that door and go after the large man to protect Nev, or run back to my car and call the police and let them handle this.

Ten seconds later, he was speaking a bit too loudly into his phone.

"You've got to get someone over here to the Sparrow house, and fast. Something is really wrong. I think someone is trying to kill the girl."

Chapter 39

May 18th 10:27 p.m.

Nev turned around on the second floor landing, and with all the strength and ferocity she could muster, yelled, "Come and get me, you psycho asshole!"

Then she dashed up the final set of steps, the narrow winding steps that connected their floor to her mom's studio. As she pushed off the first step with her left leg she winced a little.

"Stupid," she thought. "I was fine until I kicked the tweed man. It's okay though. Not injured, just hurt. I can play with pain."

The reality was you never reached the end of a game without being in some pain. While this wasn't a game by any stretch of the imagination, Nev knew this was the end. Either her plan worked and she walked out a winner, or it failed and she wouldn't be walking out at all.

Nev knew she could have just run. Every character in every horror movie ever, if they could come un-mutilated, un-murdered, would have given her the same advice: Just get as far away as fast as you can.

But she was facing three killers tonight, in her own home, and that had to mean something. These psycho idiots had shown because they wanted to kill her. They weren't looking for any random person, they each wanted her and only her.

This wasn't the sort of problem she could solve by running away. Her fate was to face this. Heck, she'd faced the other two. The Professor was in a lump on the first floor because he'd underestimated Nev. The Chrissy woman was barely able to move in the basement because she'd underestimated Nev.

Now it was this last one, this Coach. She had no intention of letting him get close enough to see if he also would underestimate her. She'd seen enough of him to know that any kind of a fight was playing to his strengths, and they looked to be fairly impressive.

But so was she. She was upstairs now, waiting. She was waiting with a plan.

She'd made her plan while racing from the basement on the back staircase into the kitchen. Nev knew you didn't win by playing to the strengths of others. This coach: He's big, so she'd slow him down in the narrow winding staircase leading to her mom's studio. He's mean, he would be coming up those stairs more slowly than he'd want. She'd never let him touch her. But the big one, she loosened the lid on her mom's almost full gallon of her special blue. It was cyan, magenta and a bit of yellow, and the chemical composition, well, it had worked once before. It was, and Nev now saw this is a good thing, heavy on the ol' Thiodiethylene glycol.

With the jar on the table overlooking the staircase, she took the time to pry the blue lid off the white bucket of pool cleaner. It wasn't all full, but the crystals still filled three quarters of the bucket.

Nev took a couple deep breaths to calm herself, then tried to count Coach's progress as he tromped up the stairs.

"Nev," his voice was deep, and strong. "I respect you for this, I really do."

He sounded as if he was coming up the first flight of steps. He sounded a bit winded, but stairs get to a lot of people.

"I'm giving you this chance to flee," she said. "You want to take my advice."

"Good girl," he answered. "I knew I picked well. The best athletes always know they can win in any situation. I pegged you as one of the best. That's why I'm here."

"You said you were going to cut off my leg, to keep. What kind of a sicko does that."

He was on the foot of the final flight of steps. Clearly though, he paused to think this through.

"You're focusing on the details, and not seeing the bigger picture," he said. "Yes, I said I need your leg, and I do. But there's a reason, a good reason. I'm hunting perfection, and only perfection. Your left leg, well, it's remarkable what you can do with it on a soccer field."

Nev knew she couldn't, or at least shouldn't, pause too long. If she wasn't continuing this chat, he'd just start climbing the steps. While she had a plan, she wasn't overly interested in setting it into action just now. She needed a few more deep breaths, at least.

"I'm not calmed by that, you know," she finally said. "I've got plans of my own for my leg."

Which is when she heard what sounded like a catch in Coach's throat.

"I know you do, Nev," he said, softly, sadly. "This is the reality of my life, of my art, of my mission, sacrifices must be made. Tragically, the sacrifices must come from the best of the best. I'm sorry that this means you, but you should be proud that it does. It means you've been blessed with greatness."

"Blessed?"

"There are no scrubs in my project. There are none of those with natural talent, but without the will to be great. You all share the natural talent, and the work ethic and the results. You're all wonderful, and when you all are combined, the pieces combine into a perfect."

"You're sick."

"I'm not the first artist to be seen as such. We're often misunderstood in our own time."

Nev could hear the creak of the first step in the spiral. "Ha," she thought, "more like in the death spiral. Keep up your sense of humor, girl!" He was climbing, again, slowly.

"So you're an artist?"
There was a pause. He was still invisible on the steps, but she'd been counting the creaks of the steps, and thought he'd come into view within one of two more steps. She was just about ready though. This guy was seriously whacko.

"I am," he said.

"But Chrissy, downstairs, she said you were a coach?"

"I am a coach. I've dedicated my life to athletics. But that is an art. My medium is young bodies. I've spent my life molding them. This project takes me the last step, to perfection, which is never possible with just one person. See, I use your left leg, and Cindy's right arm, and Jane's head, all of which were as close to perfect as humans get in their disciplines, and I combine them into a greater whole. I mold them into human perfection. It's the culmination of my life's passion. You're my last piece. You should be honored."

"I'm not, you know. You're a serial killer."

"I'm a serial artist."

"You're a psycho, just like the psycho downstairs..."

"Nev, you shouldn't resort to name calling, that's the woman I love."

"Well she started out saying she was on a mission too, a mission of mercy, but in the end she admitted she just really likes killing people."

Nev could hear that Coach had stopped. She figured he was puzzling over this in his mind. She used this time to completely remove the cap from her Mom's pot of purple, and lifted it into both hands.

Finally, she heard Coach's voice again.

"Why can't we be both, Nev? Why can't we be motivated by art, and the need to help others, as well as the desire to kill? Are we supposed to be one dimensional?"

With that he resumed creaking up the stairs. Nev had to catch her breath to hold her courage. The plan will work, the plan will work. She needed him to take one more step, at most two. She had one shot at this, and only one shot.

Staring at her, he took the next step.

"She was right, you know, you are a beauty queen."

"So do you love her?"

"I do, and when we're done here, I need to go back to her. I think we're going to be together for a long time. But I have to ask, the other one, the little professor in the tweed, was he right? Are you also smart?"

As he spoke he started to take his next step.

"You tell me," Nev shouted, raising the jar up and sending it flying down six steps at him. The jar opening was pointed directly at him, so when his arm came up to block the contents exploded out and covered him. The thick, purply liquid was clinging in wet globs to his hoodie,

214

his jeans. It was smeared on his face and neck and hands. It pooled on the steps in front, and behind him.

The attack clearly shocked him. He stopped, and looked up at her wide-eyed. It was a look of surprise, but also disappointment.

"Oh, Nev," he finally said. "Was that your best shot. I really expected better from you. I'd convinced that you were something quite special, even beyond the other donors to my project. But I guess there's a reason I didn't come for your head."

As he spoke, Nev's left arm snaked behind her and gripped the blue handle of the lidless white bucket, then slowly brought it around in front of her. She held it up in as threatening a manner as can be made with a white plastic bucket.

"Are you familiar with $(HOCH_2CH_2)_2S + 2\ HCl \rightarrow (ClCH_2CH_2)_2S + 2\ H_2O$?" she asked.

"Am I familiar with what?"

"The chemical composition for mustard gas," she said. "It's basically just a combination of Thiodiglycol, which is pretty much what's clinging to you right now, and hydrochlorid acid."

She smiled and raised the bucket a little.

The horror that registered in his eyes was a bit of a surprise for her, but before he could move, she sent a spray of crystals down the narrow stairs.

Some of the crystals flew by. Some bounced off the walls. But most stuck in the purple gloop. They stuck on his hoodie, and on his jeans. They stuck to his face and neck and hands. They covered the pools on the steps.

"The crystals," Nev said, "are almost pure hydrochloric acid."

Coach immediately began clawing at his face and neck, but it was too late. Nev saw the yellow brown smoke rising before she caught the whiff of garlic. It was only seconds before Coach fell to his knees, and then backwards, struggling to breathe.

Nev knew this place, atop a turret in a room with a single exit, and an exit that was blocked by both a chemical weapon and a psychotic killer, was not the best place to hang out. In less than a minute, she'd be gasping and retching, just like Coach was now doing.

But staying here had never been in the plan. Nev stepped back behind her Mom's easels and lifted the heavy bundle of ropes and wood that she'd spent her childhood cleaning, and wondering about.

"The rule is 'Only in a real emergency,'" she recalled. "I think this qualifies."

As the heavy bundle smashed through the windows and unfurled, she could hear the loud rasping from Coach's lungs. He was struggling back up the steps.

She wasn't overly concerned. She didn't think he'd make it too quickly.

Still, time to get moving, she thought. With the sole of her left foot, she kicked a few straggling shards of glass from the window frame, then stepped out of the window, gripping the rope and climbing down the wooden steps.

She was pleasantly surprised to see the street in front of her house was filling up with police cars. It wasn't quite a Hollywood scene. Chances didn't have that many cops to begin with. But it would do.

Chapter 40

May 18th 10:31 p.m.

EMT Martin Kingdom was in his car, berating himself for not having the courage to go into the house.

"Chicken, chicken, chicken," he said, while slapping his forehead. "That poor girl. That poor little girl, all on her own. Why didn't I go in."

He knew why, however. The guy chasing her had been huge. And there had already been a body against the door. And, well, he wasn't exactly an action hero.

Still, he couldn't get the image of that young girl running for her life up the stairs, and the ogre chasing after her.

He'd told the police, and even now they were preparing to go into the house. But they'd also seen what looked like a body at the front door. As they told him, there were ways to handle situations like this, and storming into the house before they knew what they were storming into was not the best idea.

"That's how we end up with extra bodies," he'd been told.

So there really wasn't much left for him to do right now, except sit in his car and look at the house and regret that he wasn't more of an action hero type. Which is when he heard a window smash, and saw a bright white path twist and flow down the side of the house. Looking up, at the bright light from the room at the top, which looked to be almost all glass, he watched a dark shape step out of the window and onto the white path

"Is that a ladder?" he wondered. "A rope ladder? Wow, that's cool."

And then he could clearly see Nev. The moon was lighting her perfectly, and she was almost gliding down the ladder. From the window above her, Kingdom saw smoke. It wasn't the heavy smoke of a house fire. But clearly, it was smoke, and it was rolling out in wisps and dissipating in the breeze as it seemed to flow towards Nev as she passed the second floor, and got to the first, where she lightly dropped to the ground.

Kingdom felt like applauding. It had been a beautiful sight. He thought about running over and high fiving her on escaping the intense danger that had been stalking her. He thought about that though and realized congratulating her, and celebrating with her, would mean admitting that he'd seen the danger and run away.

It would also mean wading through the cops who had also watched her descent and were now gathering around her. While they were standing, she was pointing at the window above. He couldn't make out what she was saying, but soon the cops were running away from the house and she was walking behind them.

"Man, she couldn't be any calmer," he thought.

But then the cops were waving, crazy like, and it took him a minute to realize it was directed at him. They wanted him over there? Why?

Kingdom got out of his car and walked across the street.

"What's up?"

"Can you talk at look at Ms. Sparrow?"

"Anything wrong?"

"She might have been poisoned."

"I wasn't poisoned."

"Can you make sure she's okay?"

"It was just a little bit of gas, and I was out of there before it reached me. But you should call an ambulance for the big guy. He's going to need some help. He caught a lot of the gas."

"Gas?" Kingdom asked, confused.

"Mustard gas. She did it again," a cop said, but the cop was smiling.

"Little bit of mustard gas," she added, holding her hand up and showing fingers that were about half an inch apart. "Maybe a bit more."

"Should I call an ambulance?"

"Yes," the cop said.

"You know, maybe call three," Nev added. "None of them are in very good shape right now."

"Three?"

"Yeah."

"Why?"

"Well, there are three injured people inside the house."

"Injured how?"

"Let's see, one has head and chest injuries. He may have some broken bones from being thrown down the stairs. He's somewhere around the front door."

"Holy crap?"

"Another has some pretty serious facial cuts and a concussion. She's in the middle room in the basement."

"Wow, really."

"And the third is having trouble breathing, you know, from the mustard gas? He probably also has some serious bruises because I think I heard him falling down the steps."

"What the fuck happened in there?"

"Oh, they're the three serial killers who came to murder me."

"Uh huh, So… What?"

"They didn't win. I won."

"Holy shit. You okay?"

"I'm fine. They need a bit of looking after."

Chapter 41

May 19th 11:34 a.m.

When Brody finally woke up the next morning, Nev was sitting in a chair by the side of his bed at the Liberty Hospital. It had been an easy commute, as the police the night before insisted she be taken in for observation overnight. She'd been in a room directly above Brody, and there had been a lot of showers, like six. The doctors had ordered her clothes removed and destroyed.

Nev had told them it was pointless.

"I wasn't exposed to the mustard gas. At least, not much of it."

This assurance of hers had failed to impress the doctors. But first thing this morning, a nice nurse had run over to Target and returned with neon orange sweat pants, some orange Crocs which her mother might wear and a Denver Broncos tee-shirt. A lot of orange, but comfy enough. After breakfast, having the basics of something to wear, she'd walked to a nearby Wal-Mart and bought some jeans and everything else she was going to need for the next several days (using Bro's credit card).

After making her exit from the house, the night before was a bit of a blur. The house was bathed in blue and red flashing light.

The cops came over to talk to her about what had gone on inside, and she'd repeated the story, though with more details as they had a lot of questions.

When she was done explaining the situation, the cops put on Hazmat suits. She thought the suits made them look as if they were Space Cops. They went into the house with their guns drawn. In order, they dragged out the man in tweed who was mumbling in Latin, but hadn't been exposed to the gas (which was good, Nev thought, as she didn't like the idea of having trashed the entire house. She imagined the reaction if her Mom and Dad had come home to find the house bulldozed, and laughed, then panicked a little). He was groggy and placed on a stretcher, which he was then handcuffed to. As Kingdom and the newly arrived EMT rolled the Professor by her, the madman mumbled something about "failed, failed like all of them did." Exactly who he was referring to was difficult to tell.

"Not me," she thought. "I'm still here. I passed."

Next the police walked out Coach. They had him in cuffs, and he was huge as she remembered, but now also red and rashy, and he stopped to vomit once. She knew he had intended to kill her, but she still felt a little guilty about gassing him. It was, after all, kind of a war crime.

But he was walking in front of the Space Cops, and when he saw her across the street, he called "Good game, Nev. I wasn't expecting a science nerd."

Later she'd learn that it wasn't anything close to a weapons grade mustard gas, more like mustard gassy. Still, it wasn't good to have been exposed.

Finally, they'd actually wheeled out Chrissy. They said they'd tried to walk her out, and she first collapsed, then attacked them. So Chrissy was restrained in a wheelchair, and she looked both really beaten up and super angry. She didn't say anything that Nev could hear as they rolled her by, just scowled. "Yikes," Nev said when she met Chrissy's eyes, and at that a smile flickered onto Chrissy's face.

"Yeah, she's full blown crazy," Nev thought.

All three were loaded into ambulances, each complete with a pair of police officers.

Now, sitting on a chair next to Bro's hospital bed, and playing with the tablet that the office had leant her, she'd hoped that moment, when the ambulances pulled away, sirens going, lights flashing, was officially how the nightmare would end.

Of course, it hadn't. First, she had to be decontaminated. Then she learned that the same chemical weapons expert who'd come to her school years ago was now at her house, and people in moon suits were hauling away a ton of stuff to a Hazmat incinerator. She'd been told she'd be staying in a motel for at least a week.

It would be another couple days before her Mom and Dad had Wi-Fi in the Maldives, so that part of the nightmare, telling them, was yet to come.

Disturbingly, the three suspects were all actually in this same hospital right now being treated. She'd overheard the cops say that only Coach would be staying for more than the one night, but that it looked like he was going to get through with some nasty scars and not much else. The other two were on their way to the county jail halfway between here and Chances.

Officially, the cops had told her that she'd have to testify against all three. One had whispered that it wouldn't matter so much with Coach. While waiting for the Hazmat suits the night before, they'd noticed the remarkably quiet hum of a generator coming from a camper van across the street and a quarter block down from her house. The generator, he said, was running a deep freeze in the camper van.

"You aren't going to believe what we found," he said. "I couldn't tell you if I wanted, but you'd never believe it anyway."

"It was basically a complete girl, made up of the parts of lots of girls, but missing a left leg," Nev said.

"What? How'd you know that?"

"He told me he needed my left leg. I was the last piece of his puzzle."

"Man, oh man, I didn't think that was possible, but that's even grosser. I gotta tell the detectives."

After that, her morning had been sitting and waiting, playing Bejeweled on the tablet and watching the television news reports of what had happened to her. It was amazing how little the reporters actually knew about it all. The reporters on CNN and Fox News knew less than the local ones, which she found surprising.

So she was quite ready when Bro finally stirred.

"Nev? Nev, you're here? You're okay?"

"Yeah, I'm just fine."

"Uh, where is here?"

"Hospital. Colorado. You had a car crash."

"Oh God, I was trying to get to you. Something happened to you. I remember a scream, just before the accident."

"Yeah, no big deal. I'm fine. I think, though, I found the psychos you were looking for."

"You found them?"

"Well, they found me. They were all at the house last night."

"All of them?"

"Yep."

"And..."

"They're all in police custody now."

"What happened?"

"I did. I told you, I'm a bit of a badass."

She laughed, and Bro laughed. Then he shook his head.

"You really had three people at the house last night trying to kill you?"

"Yep."

"And you think they were the ones I was talking about earlier in the day?"

"They sure seem like the same psychos."

"Wow."

"Good thing you flew out to protect me. If you hadn't come out, who knows what would have happened," she said, and laughed a little.

"Okay, I get it. Yes, you are a bit of a badass. And you really think it was the cases I'm looking into?"

"A Professor who goes after smart kids, a Coach who chases athletes, and a freaky woman who hunts beauty queens. That sound like them?"

"Wow, it really does. They showed up on the same night and you were all of what they hunted in one package."

"Yeah, wow. I mean, what are the odds."

The End

The End

Made in the USA
Middletown, DE
23 October 2020

22588944R00139